P9-CEL-160

CONTENTS

Tired with all these, for restful death I cry
Znaven tím vším, já chci jen smrt a klid,
As, to behold desert a beggar born,
jen nevidět, jak žebrá poctivec,
And needy nothing trimm'd in jollity,
Jak pýchou dme se pouhý parazit,
And purest faith unhappily forsworn ...
jak pokřiví se každá dobrá věc,
...Tired with all these, from these would I be gone,
... Znaven tím vším, já chci být, lásko, v hrobě,
Save that, to die, I leave my love alone.
jen nemuset tím sbohem dát i tobě.

William Shakespeare
Sonnet LXVI
Translated by Martin Hilský

To Václav Havel

Farrar, Straus and Giroux
19 Union Square West, New York 10003

Copyright © 2001 by Josef Škvorecký
All rights reserved
Printed in the United States of America
Originally published in 1999 by Key Porter Books, Canada
Published in the United States by Farrar, Straus and Giroux
First American edition, 2001

Library of Congress Cataloging-in-Publication Data
Škvorecký, Josef.
   Two murders in my double life / Josef Škvorecký.— 1st American ed.
    p. cm.
  ISBN 0-374-28025-8 (hardcover : alk. paper)
   1. College teachers—Fiction.   2. Women publishers—Fiction.
3. Married people—Fiction.   4. Czechoslovakia—Fiction.
5. Immigrants—Fiction.   6. Canada—Fiction.   I. Title.
PR9199.3.S545 T9 2001
813'.54—dc21

00-049516

Designed by Peter Maher

TWO MURDERS
IN MY DOUBLE LIFE

Josef Škvorecký

Farrar, Straus and Giroux

New York

Two Murders
in My Double Life

My thanks to

Doris Cowan, Patrick Crean, Ed Galligan, Anna Porter,

Sam Solecki, and Derek Weiler

Before the Story Begins

To be an exile is, in some ways, to be a split personality. The longer one lives in a foreign country, the farther away one feels from the old homeland, and the fonder one gets of the new one. However, the old country never disappears beyond the horizon, and the new one, to the exile, will never become the open book that it is to those who were born there, and can read it with no difficulty.

The story is about that, about isolation in paradise, but it is mainly about murder in two locations. The two parts represent two different literary genres, really. Edenvale College looks much like a "guilty vicarage," as W. H. Auden used to call such things. The events in Prague are pure old-fashioned realism, which to foreigners may seem surreal, and they are about a total crime.

North America leads, by a wide margin, in the worldwide statistics of murder, but North Americans have never experienced total crime. In Europe and Asia, millions of people fell victim to it, many millions in large countries, but it is not only the body that is murdered by this mega-assassin, it is the soul: the character of the community called a nation. However, one can hardly write a murder mystery about the assassination of souls. That's why the Edenvale story has all the paraphernalia of the guilty vicarage, but the Prague sequence of events lacks them entirely. Its characters, as the narrator says, are not in a detective story written for the entertainment of the reader, but in a very serious novel.

J.S.

Two Murders

in My Double Life

Two of the Many Girls in My Life, and My Wife

FROM MY OFFICE, through the open door, I could see into his office across the hall. There he was, the star of our college, grooming his Clark Gable–like moustache with a small comb and looking into a hand mirror. Then my view was obstructed by a girl's back in a Gucci jacket. Not that I am so knowledgeable about women's fashion, but when I commented on her great looks in the new outfit, she just smiled and said, "Gucci." Some girls at our college would resent my male admiration, but she was above parroting current wisdoms. Her blond hair was freshly coiffured and shiny, and reached her shoulders in lovely waves. Her name was Candace Quentin. She was our college beauty queen.

I managed to get a glimpse of her elegant legs beneath a black, knee-length skirt, and then all these objects of interest vanished behind the closing door. A sign in gold on black

3

announced that the room was the sanctuary of Professor James F. Cooper.

This was very unusual. Ever since the college had distributed the "Sexual Harassment" pamphlet for the edification of male staff members, office doors (unless a woman sat behind them) remained ajar. Whenever some girl student thoughtlessly shut the door behind her in a male professor's office, the professor immediately opened it again.

Cooper did no such thing. I looked at my wristwatch, and kept track of the time she was in there. I glanced over at brief intervals for a whole quarter of an hour. The door stayed shut. After eighteen minutes a bespectacled student, his white, serious face filled with apprehension, appeared in the hall and knocked at the door, very timidly. Cooper probably could not hear the pianissimo knock, and his door did not open. With extreme caution, the bespectacled student turned the knob slowly, and peered in. Then, in a loud whisper, he blurted, "Oh, I beg your pardon, Professor Cooper! I'll come later." From behind the door, Cooper commanded, "Come tomorrow, Browning!" The young man murmured, "Yes, professor!" and meekly withdrew. During this curt exchange I did not manage to get even a peep at what was going on inside. I was curious, because Cooper had always been very punctilious about observing the rules laid down in the harassment brochure. I continued to consult my watch at brief intervals for the next ten minutes.

Suddenly Police Sergeant Dorothy Sayers barged in unannounced, apparently hoping against hope that she would be able to corner me in my office.

As a rule, I was not to be found there. I preferred to hold tutorials at the college pub, the Lame Duck. But this time

Sayers was lucky, and immediately pressed her advantage. Instead of watching Cooper's gold-and-black name plate, I was forced to give part of my attention to this policewoman, who was also my student. Now and then I tried to squint over her shoulder at Cooper's closed door. Just as she finished delivering her report about her "Locked Room" project—with the words "I'm at my wits' end, professor!"—the door flew open and out came a teary Candace Quentin. She actually ran out and down the hall without closing the door. I had never seen her like that: she was a proud, self-assured goddess. Was it possible that her tears were the result of some amorous disappointment? With the user of a moustache comb? Come on!

It turned out later, as I delved into the mystery of our local murder, that I was right to doubt that interpretation.

Inside, I could see Cooper now; he picked up a journal and stuck a pipe into his mouth. The pipe remained unlit, because under pressure from environmentalist groups the Dean had declared our building "smoke-free."

Baffled by the mystery of the closed door, my mind wandered back to Police Sergeant Sayers as she droned on about the Mystery of the Locked Room. This was a topic I'd given to students of my seminar on writing detective stories; it called for devising and solving the problem of a murder victim found in a room from which the perpetrator has inexplicably vanished, but which is locked on the inside, with the key still in the lock.

THE TWO GIRLS, QUENTIN AND SAYERS, HAD ENROLLED in my seminar for different reasons, misguided in each case. Quentin assumed that my seminar would be a Mickey-Mouse course, and so she chose it over "Shakespeare's Historical Plays" or "Restoration Comedy," in both of which the students had to write four papers per semester, and a scholarly approach was required and enforced. All Quentin needed was one more English course, because her major was science, or to be precise, mathematics, which she studied with Cooper across the hall. Sayers, on the other hand, took my course on the pretext of adding an original perspective to her courses in criminology, which she took for her career in police work. In actual fact Sayers was in love with me.

The two girls—I call them girls, because even though I have been told over and over that they are women, to me they still look like girls—were as different as their reasons for choosing my seminar. Quentin was a glorious blonde, the daughter of a rich entrepreneur; Sayers, on the other hand, was a sergeant in the Mississauga police department, who regularly jogged to the college from the precinct station because she was overweight.

Only slightly overweight—but it struck me that a conviction of one's own obesity was a widespread female malady. Even the slender Quentin, when once I found her in the cafeteria eating fat-free yogurt, had told me that she had to shed five pounds. Why she had to do such an unnecessary thing was a mystery to me. I figured that shedding five pounds would make Candace almost skeletal.

Sayers was unequivocally after me; she was not bothered by the fact that I was married, and could not understand why the existence of a wife should be an obstacle. As for my wife, she easily recognized Queen Candace of Edenvale College in the heroine of the little crime novel I was writing at the time, but she wasn't bothered either. She liked to listen to my stories about my maiden students, and I was fond of telling them. My wife, Sidonia, was a wise woman, and in spite of her old-fashioned name she held quite modern views. Or, rather, she was just wise. She saw through me like a piece of glass, and knew that I did not take my female students seriously as sexual objects. The Professor of Women's Studies, Ann Kate Boleyn, did *not* understand me, and was very suspicious: I had caught that scholar several times watching me when I was watching girls. But Sidonia knew that although I wrote only crime stories, I was a poet at heart, like my hero Raymond Chandler, and pretty young females were for me, well, not quite what Professor Boleyn thought. It was just that—to echo Hemingway's hero in "Soldier's Home"—they made such a nice pattern. That's why Sidonia didn't mind even the lovesick attacks of Sergeant Sayers, about which I kept her posted, because she liked hearing about them. She knew what she knew about me.

AND I KNEW WHAT I KNEW ABOUT HER. I KNEW HOW IT had been, forty years before in Prague, when she told me that an agent of the state police, the StB, was pestering her. That was how I knew what I knew about the List of StB informers, which after the fall of Communism was clandestinely leaked to the naive, or more likely vile, Mr. Mrkvicka, and printed in his weekly paper *Kill Kommunism!* Nor was it a mystery to me why the agents leaked the List.

Unfortunately, my wife was on the List, and despite her wisdom, she succumbed to a deadly depression. The trumped-up charges came shortly after the world-renowned playwright, who was now president of the country, had awarded her the Order of the White Lion, for her twenty-five years of publishing drudgery in Toronto. The publishing house was her brainchild; she had rescued from oblivion many manuscripts that had been silenced by Communist censors in Prague. Among them were those the world-renowned playwright had kept producing—between incarcerations.

Due to historical events, however, Sidonia's publishing activities eventually became redundant. Then Mr. Mrkvicka subjected them to an unexpected interpretation. In an article called "Put Your Cards on the Table, Mrs. Sidonia!" he divulged her secret career: she had been a lifelong agent of the StB; in fact, she had married me on orders from her StB bosses, to keep me under round-the-clock surveillance. As a writer who kept concocting crime stories modelled on American thrillers, I was regarded by the Party with keen suspicion. For that same reason, on orders from above, Sidonia drew me with her into exile in Canada, where she launched her publishing business: a front, of course, so that the StB would have control over emigré publications. Her publishing lists were always submitted to the Central Committee of the Communist Party for their okay. The article further revealed that Sidonia flew regularly and secretly to Prague, to report to her StB bosses.

Czech wisdom has it that there is a grain of truth in every piece of nonsense. According to this maxim, the slight admixture of the genuine gives even the boldest feats of imagination the ring of authenticity. Anonymous letters soon began to arrive, recommending that Sidonia leave Toronto. After Mr. Mrkvicka's revelations and the publication of several addenda to the evil lore of the List in his paper, Sidonia's old Prague friend Julie wrote us that the only way to disprove the accusation was to sue the Ministry of the Interior. We were waiting at the airport before boarding a plane to Prague when Jirousek, a member of the Toronto branch of the Association of Political Prisoners of the Communist Regime, approached us and rolled up his sleeve to show Sidonia scars from cigarette burns on his forearm. "This is how the StB worked me over," he said, "while you were working for them."

I thought Sidonia would die of shame. However, by incessantly buzzing into her ear throughout the flight to Prague that I knew what I knew about it, and that it was all lies, I kept her alive.

In the Prague Film Club we ran into an obscure actor called Emil Konrad, who after the Velvet Revolution had appointed himself "Earl" and added "of Hradek" to his surname. He almost finished Sidonia off when he stage-whispered to his female companion for everybody to hear, "Why doesn't this StB moll stay put in Canada?" Looking at Sidonia, as she sat next to the Earl at the bar, the image of Poe's murdered Marie Roget, drawn from the Seine, occurred to me for the first time. Her face had just the same deadly pallor as that of the poor, raped and murdered cigar girl from Mr. Anderson's store, on whom Poe modelled the French heroine of his gruesome story.

Naturally, my colleagues at Edenvale College had no idea what was going on. We lived in two very different worlds, and they only knew their own.

CHAPTER TWO

How I Gave a Lift to One of the Girls in My Life

COOPER WAS THE STAR of our college because he had been nominated for the Nobel Prize, but there was no Nobel Prize for mathematics, and Cooper's discovery touched on physics only marginally, and so he failed to gain the honour. But even without the prize he made the college and himself world-famous, on account of something named "Cooper's theorem," which was well beyond my mathematical expertise. I thought it had something to do with putting the acausality of microcosm back into the causal nexus, or perhaps it caught Einstein—or was it Darwin?—in some error. In any case the result was, again for reasons incomprehensible to me, that Cooper became for a short time a hero to the Christian fundamentalists.

He had always been a windbag, but his global fame blew him up to the size of a Goodyear blimp. I once addressed him in the faculty club with a seriously meant question (though I framed my inquiry as a joke) of whether he intended to fail our college's prettiest student on the grounds of her "lookism" (the feminist sin of caring for one's looks). In my class, I protested, she was very capable and industrious, despite being beautiful. He pompously responded that feminist categories had nothing to do with the fact that Quentin was a mathematical illiterate, and he saw no reason why, if she deserved it, he shouldn't give her an F.

Once, over a whisky, my colleague McMountain told me that, according to his students, the "F" in James F. Cooper didn't just stand for "Fenimore." McMountain's speciality was CanLit and in the past ten years—the length of my acquaintance with him—he had lived with three or four budding Canadian female novelists, who invariably became the subjects of his seminars. About the life and work of two of them he wrote scholarly books, and despite an impressive critical apparatus they were more than readable, their attraction due to inside information and a fast-paced style based on the American hard-boiled school. However, since few CanLit critics were conversant with the stylistic theories of that more-than-usually-bloody faction of American letters, McMountain was highly praised as a stylistic innovator of scholarly writing.

But I had my doubts about that knowing interpretation of Cooper's middle initial. Our mathematical star did not strike me as a violator of young virgins. Or maybe he just kept it a well-hidden secret; I remembered Candace's tears. Rumours also went around that Cooper was queer, but no names of intimate friends of that kind were mentioned.

MY CHAT WITH COOPER IN THE FACULTY CLUB, DURING which I made my joke about his grading intentions, reminded me that only a few days before I had described Candace's tears to Wendy McFarlane, my favourite Irish redhead and private college spy. She insisted that I had misinterpreted what I saw. "Your mistake," Wendy told me. "She has nothing going on with Cooper. F-13 gave her Fs for all her papers, and it looks like she is going to fail his course unless she cheats success-fully—very successfully, that is—on her final exam. Which is as likely as me becoming the Archbishop of Canterbury." "F-13" was Cooper's nickname, after the popular horror films, all called *Friday the 13th*, which dealt with the horrible deaths of female college students.

"Why would she care so much?" I wondered. I knew from a recent poll in *Maclean's* that Candace's father was the forty-ninth richest man in Canada, and so she did not depend on good grades for a student loan.

"Quentin wants to get into law school," Wendy explained, "and she'll have to take an exam in math. If F-13 gives her a final F, they won't even let her try."

That seemed reasonable. But why did she close the door of Cooper's office, a strict no-no at Edenvale? Wasn't it perhaps Wendy who was mistaken about the beauty queen and her math instructor? Was Candace weeping because the windbag had told her, probably in the same tone he used with me at the faculty club, that as far as her grades were concerned there was nothing to discuss? But with what arguments could she possibly appeal to him, when Fs on all her previous papers hinted clearly what his response would be? Candace, the cool princess of Edenvale?

"Beats me," said Wendy, "but it was certainly not what your dirty mind made you think, professor. I know Candace better than anyone. From church."

My favourite freckled spy was studying to be an Anglican priestess.

THAT NIGHT, AS WE WERE DRIVING HOME FROM PROFESSOR Kelly's party, another strange scene was played out. As always, Kelly overindulged. Sidonia did likewise, though not as much, and her reasons were better than his. Kelly was fond of whisky, pure and simple, and liked to give lavish parties (financed by his wealthy wife) for the sake of overindulging in convivial company. Over the years, parties at Kelly's had become monotonous, with nothing remarkable about them except the free access to spirits. This time, however, the foreseeable event had an unexpected sequel, which stuck in my mind.

It was shortly after midnight, and the night was standard horror-movie footage. Thunder, lightning, and ferocious wind. We were passing Professor Mather's Victorian mansion, and I remarked to my wife that it loomed like the Bates motel in *Psycho*. Sidonia just muttered something about everything reminding me of the movies, and on that point she was right. A long, long time ago my father managed the local cinema in Kostelec, and I practically spent my youth in his movie house. The experiences of youth determine the rest of our lives. I'm not sure how valid this *aperçu* is for others, but it fully applies to me.

Suddenly, a girl's figure wavered into the beam of my headlights and I stepped on the brakes. She turned, putting up her hand to shade her eyes from the glare. It was Quentin. I opened my door and stepped outside into the rain.

13

"My God, what are you doing here?"

She stared at me wildly, and perhaps because everything reminded me of the movies, I saw the face of the heroine of the latest installment of *Friday the 13th*, having just escaped the knife of the indestructible killer.

I opened the rear door of the car for her and without a second's hesitation she jumped in. Once safely tucked into the back seat, she relaxed, and the horror, or whatever it was, vanished from her face. Perhaps it was only dismay over the wetting of her freshly styled hair.

What was she doing here alone, at night, in a violent storm?

She immediately offered an explanation. "My car stalled over on Cresthill, and the phone in the booth was out of order. So I started walking. I thought if anybody came along they would give me a lift."

That sounded logical. To ask what she was doing on Cresthill would be impolite, because she was an adult and could do whatever she pleased.

"What were you doing on Cresthill?" my wife asked.

"I was at a terribly boring party."

"Who throws terribly boring parties at Edenvale?" I asked.

"Would you believe it? I didn't know them," she said with a tiny echo of irony. "I ended up there with some girls who'd been dancing at the Lame Duck. I don't even know who they were. I think they're from Scarborough somewhere."

"Must've been a remarkable party," I said with the same echo of irony. "You didn't recognize anybody?"

I wasn't asking for any particular reason. It just struck me as odd that the beauty queen of the Edenvale campus, the most popular girl in those parts, had ended up at a party among total strangers.

"Oh, well, there were a few guys from Edenvale, Freddie Hamilton, I think Wayne—no, he wasn't there. I seem to remember Lorraine Henderson. But I couldn't swear by it. Mainly it was all terribly boring."

We crossed the bridge over the Mississauga rivulet and approached the campus. The Hollywood storm was still raging.

"Where shall I drop you?" I asked.

"Dorm 15-A, if you please."

I first became acquainted with Quentin when she decided to take my course in the writing of detective stories. Unlike some other students, she wasn't foolish enough to believe that such a skill could be taught: she just wanted an easy credit. In the car I wondered again why the beautiful and by no means dense daughter of the forty-ninth richest man in Canada was not at Harvard instead of at Edenvale College—which, for all its qualities, was nothing like the Ivy League, and not just because it was a Canadian institution. The explanation was simple: Edenvale was Dad's alma mater, because at the time of his studies there in business and commerce, Dad was far from rich. Like many North Americans, he harboured sentimental feelings for his not-so-old school, even though he was now the richest man in Winnipeg.

Quentin, wet as a puppy, disappeared in the dorm gate. Sidonia lit a cigarette, and with an exaggerated sigh said, "What a nice plot for your next trashy novel! Your beautiful student has just committed a murder."

"I'm sure she has a waterproof alibi."

"I wouldn't swear by that girl's alibis," said Sidonia.

NOT LONG BEFORE, AND IN LESS DRAMATIC WEATHER, I had driven down Cresthill with Vojtech Kysely. Normally, I wouldn't care for his company, but he called me when word spread that my wife was editing an anthology of articles by people who had been falsely included in Mr. Mrkvicka's List. Rumours change so much going from one person to the next that by the time it reached Kysely he had got the impression that Sidonia intended to publish a book about informers, and he offered to talk to her. "Talk to her about what?" I asked him, and without a trace of embarrassment he told me that before emigrating to Canada, he had been a colonel in the state security forces.

I agreed to meet him in the Czech pub on Golf Club Road, and he spoke of his deeds as if they had been innocent everyday occurrences. Horror crept up my spine. By way of introduction he sketched out his life story for me: an orphan in a poor village in the Moravian mountains, joined the guerillas at fourteen, etc., all the way to the turning point of his miserable but heroic life: "You're a proletarian, comrade. Join the Party!" A believable motivation. The orphan accepted the offer, but he was intelligent, and some sort of moral residue clung to his conscience, perhaps from having been an altar boy in his youth (as he had also told me). When the Party chairman Dubcek attempted to put a human face on Bolshevism—which is about as possible as squaring a circle—in 1968, he had been sick of it all for some time, and defected to Canada. Here, after the initial screening, which lasted a month and included interviews with interested agents of the FBI, he was given a new name and eventually did well. He became an entrepreneur with his own company; his son and daughter had graduated from university, and both were married now.

O, Canada, our home, not exactly *native,* but still *our land!* You generous haven for anybody! You unreal land over the rainbow! In the pub where the incredible self-made man acquainted me with his c.v., I felt like intoning the anthem.

Instead of singing, though, I just listened. At the end of Kysely's two-hour monologue I still did not know what it was he had been so sick of. He talked of his former police work not exactly with enthusiasm, but with an air of keen interest in the technical details, the way Doc McCormick had explained the mechanics of hip-replacement surgery to me before he put me on the operating table. Kysely's stories made my mind reel, although we were drinking only instant coffee, and in the end I remembered only one of them in all its awful detail.

"... Eventually, she became our best agent," said Kysely, putting a satisfied full stop to the complicated history of Mrs. Kopanec.

Her story began in the following way: in the fifties, the famous Czech composer Septimus had lost an only son. Kysely, who brown-nosed the composer as part of his professional duties, and also because he felt flattered by the friendship of the famous man, offered his sympathy. Septimus sighed: "Oh, well ... I still have my other two boys. I haven't lost everything."

So far as anybody knew, the dead boy had been the *only* son of the widowed Septimus. That was strange. But in spite of allegedly having two more boys, Septimus grew sentimental over the dead one, and Kysely made expert use of his grief. He was a professional, and from the weepy ramblings of the depraved composer he soon deduced that the two other siblings' mother was not Septimus's deceased wife, but the spouse of a trusting friend: Josef Kopanec, the popular novelist.

Ilona Kopanec must have loved her husband, because when Kysely left for Canada, the two were still married. However, when their marriage had lasted for seven years and no children came, Ilona confided in her husband's best friend, Septimus, about how very much she and her husband yearned for a baby. The natural consequences of this initially tearful tête-à-tête were the composer's two sons, who survived their half-brother.

Ilona's husband was a very potent man, but to explain his infertile potency in logical medical terms never crossed his mind. Being a male of the old-fashioned sort, he blamed Ilona. She went to see a famous gynecologist, and brought his report home in writing: she was definitely not to blame. Even then Kopanec refused to have himself examined, and when soon afterwards the first of the two babies was born, he felt no suspicion, only vindication.

And Kysely, who had extracted this story from Septimus at a moment of the composer's weakness, took a professional attitude to the information. As he explained: "When we confronted Mrs. Kopanec with the facts, she fainted. But afterwards she was malleable like Plasticine. Eventually, she became our best agent."

He figured correctly that Ilona, whose devotion to her husband was that of a lovelorn damsel of romantic fiction, would rather do anything then let her husband know the truth. Not that she would be afraid of him, of course. But she would rather die than hurt his feelings. And she yearned for the babies so much.

In non-socialist terms, the whole affair was pure blackmail. And that was that. From Kysely, no trace of remorse or even uneasiness. Not a glimmer of anything like a revulsion serious enough to make him abandon a lucrative career for the uncertainties of exile in a foreign country across the big pond.

BEFORE I WENT TO BED THAT NIGHT, AND AFTER I HAD made sure that Sidonia was asleep, I tiptoed to her studio. Next to her word processor, in a neat pile, was her new, still unfinished novel, which she had stopped writing when Mr. Mrkvicka published his document. Under the manuscript, I knew, she kept that printed matter suitable only for use in the washroom during shortages of toilet paper. That was how Sidonia's old friend, the playwright who was now president, had characterized the List—however, although he was a popular man, a substantial portion of the nation did not agree with him on this point. The List was too tempting a morsel for gossip, especially since Sidonia, although well known, was far less famous than some of the others whose names it desecrated.

But when the List first appeared we didn't even know that Sidonia was on it. We lived in Canada, far away from such monstrous things. I wasn't interested at all in that piece of printed slander. When some so-called friends phoned to tell me that my dear friend Lester was there, too, that very fact alone made me distrust the rag.

I never believed in the conspiracy theories that were popular (particularly among those who disagreed with the president), because such theories were a veritable heaven for gossipmongers. But I reached a conclusion based on my own extensive experience with the Party-government, and for me, it shed light on the matter. Of course, I shared those experiences with the entire nation, yet many did not see the light I saw. Why? I was a crime writer, and unlike many of my non-writing compatriots I remembered a certain legal maxim. It was usually the starting point when, before the bliss of actual writing, I grappled with the unpleasant drudgery of devising a convincing motive for the murder plot.

Cui bono.

In this case the answer was simple: the publication of the List helped the so-called workers' movement, by which euphemistic description the Party camouflaged its activities. Once the List had appeared in print, the public lost interest in the five hundred or so Czech and Slovak unfortunates who had ended up on the workers' movement's gallows in the fifties. The public, with gusto, became immersed in the game of Who Is on the List, and since Party members—except the expelled Dubcekists—were not there on principle, the political aim of the leakage was achieved. To have been a Communist in the scoundrel times of the recent past was suddenly no longer such a shame. The shame was shifted to the Party's various victims, now all forced to stand on the pillory of public disgrace.

The Communists have always been excellent psychologists when it comes to dirty intrigue.

I hated the document. But that night in Sidonia's studio, I lifted the disgusting pages from under the manuscript of her novel; until then I could truthfully claim that I had not sunk so low as to look for anyone's name on the List. But I had to know whether or not a certain story had been only the bragging fantasy of a former security man. I leafed through the pages, found the letter K. She was there. Kopanec, Ilona, code name "Ilocka," born 19 August 1920 in Humpolec.

Yet Sidonia Smiricky was there, too, and she—

It was then that the bitter truth hit me: the List was a cocktail of fact and falsification.

Absurdly but clearly, I remembered my beloved horror writer, H. P. Lovecraft. Throughout his fictions he quotes from a smattering of strange books. Some are his inventions—*The Necronomicon, De Vermis Mysteriis, Unaussprechliche Kulten*—and some are books of genuine learning—Frazer's *The Golden Bough*, a rich source for T. S. Eliot's imagination, or Murray's *The Witch Cults in Western Europe*. An old, proven method: the genuine stuff adds credibility to the invented. Mr. Mrkvicka's List, however, unlike *At the Mountains of Madness*, was not used for the honourable purpose of readers' spine-chilling enjoyment.

I closed the printed pages, put them back underneath my wife's incomplete novel, and went to bed.

I didn't sleep much that night.

CHAPTER THREE

What My Clever But Sad Wife Noticed in the Common Room of Edenvale College

S IDONIA WAS A TRUE WOMAN, with nothing androgenous about her. She had all the tenderness, all the intuitiveness, that is expected of a true woman. And she noticed things.

The departments of English and mathematics celebrated the end of every semester with a party in the common room, since both departments were on the same corridor. Staff members' wives would bring an American specialty called cookies, which the students, conditioned by childhood habits, liked and ate almost non-stop. But since the cookies were common sweet biscuits, I, conditioned in childhood by the Sunday sweetshop lineups where people used to buy enormous quantities of delectable rum tarts and cream-filled wafers, wouldn't touch them. The professors' wives (never the lady professors) supposedly went to the trouble of baking the cookies themselves. "Is that so?" wondered my perceptive wife Sidonia. "So how come they always bring them in boxes marked 'Cakemaster'?"

When, many years ago, we went to our first end-of-term party, Sidonia took the innocent deceits of the profs' wives at face value and made a *Pischingertorte*; she found the special wafers from which a real *Pischinger* is made—after searching all over Toronto with no success—in Heidelberg (Ontario). The *Pischinger* became a departmental legend. Sidonia was quite a devotee of the culinary arts, and the success of her sweet artefact appealed to her patriotic feelings. It was spoiled, though, by the fact that *Pischinger* was a German tart, and so she developed the habit of bringing to the department's parties alternately *kolache* (to use the term known in Chicago), and marmalade-filled doughnut-like concoctions for which there is no English word, not even in Illinois. She got a recipe from her great-aunt Mrs. Slepitchka in the Czech village of Yukon (Oklahoma).

After the last party, some months before, she had asked me whether the playboy in the turtleneck sweater was really Raymond Hammett, the husband of Mary Mather, who kept her maiden name because she was descended from the Salem Mathers, renowned for witch-burning.

"Sidonia! Don't tell me you fell for him?"

"You bet I did! I'm a woman after all, and every woman must swoon before Hammett."

"I'll kill him!" I promised in a jolly tone, having no idea of what would happen soon.

Sidonia asked, "Why would you risk the gallows? Some woman will do that for you. Most likely one of your students."

I knew that the last Canadian executioner had retired many years ago, and I would not risk the gallows. Nevertheless, I asked, "Are you sure, Sidonia?"

"Absolutely. And to set your mind at ease, I asked about him not because I intend to succumb to his manly charms. I just wanted to know whether he is Professor Mather's husband, because he was holding hands under the table with one of your disciples—whose name, I think, is Lorraine Henderson. Which is something husbands of professors normally don't do. Or do they?"

I told Sidonia I never did it. Although in fact I quite fancied Lorraine Henderson. She was a spectacular specimen with a headful of Titian hair, cared for every third day by the owner of the Vidal Sassoon franchise in Sandbridge Mall; she spent about two hundred bucks weekly on her coiffure. No problem for her, since in the previously mentioned *Maclean's* poll her daddy had placed much higher than Candace's: as the twenty-seventh richest man in Canada. Once Lorraine forgot a fashion catalogue in my office; I took it home and Sidonia, for three days, lay absorbed in its colourful pages. It was obviously mailed only to select addresses, because as Sidonia informed me, the cheapest item listed was gentlemen's house slippers made of python skin, for four hundred and fifty dollars. The most expensive creation was an evening dress priced at sixty thousand. Why that scanty piece of rag was so costly remained a mystery to me. But at least, thanks to the careless Lorraine Henderson, we both got a glimpse of the lifestyle of the fifty richest men in Canada.

Then Mr. Mrkvicka printed his List, and Sidonia fell into deep depression. At first, she refused to attend the next department party, but I insisted, thinking that if Sidonia mixed with people who knew only their own world, she would cheer up. However, the chief topic discussed at the party was the tragedy that had struck our colleague Mather a few days before.

Perhaps it was a tragedy. In any case, it was a crime. Mather's husband Raymond Hammett got himself murdered.

In the common room, Sidonia's face grew sadder. Gloomily she viewed the assembled academics, who put on serious faces to show that they were deeply moved by the loss of one of our circle, although in actual fact they were barely able to suppress their joy at another semester's end.

At the opposite end of the table, Cooper was bragging about some honour that had recently been bestowed on him by the oldest university of the Anglo-American world. He appeared at the party in a jacket made of Harris tweed, bought at Harrods of London; its buttons resembled miniature soccer balls. Next to him sat Candace Quentin, who not so long ago had run from his office in tears. Today she looked very pleased with herself, and even grinned when Cooper blew himself up to the bursting point about his honorary degree from Albion. Nor did she show any ill effects from having been drenched to the skin recently, except perhaps that her nose had a slightly reddish tint. That I noted, because Quentin was such a pretty doll. Some much more important things wholly escaped me.

Cooper stopped bragging to catch his breath, and at that moment Sidonia leaned over across the table, grabbed one of his soccer balls and said, *"Men!"* Cooper remained puffed up for a moment, then slowly deflated, and Quentin looked at

Sidonia with surprise-filled eyes. I felt a sting of apprehension about the percentage of alcohol in my wife's veins, but in the ensuing silence she just jerked at Cooper's button and pulled it loose. "It was hanging by one thread," she explained at home, and I, the notorious author of detective stories, felt a prick of shame for my failure to notice things, unless they were young persons of the opposite sex. "Apparently, he sewed it on himself," said Sidonia. "Well, what can one expect from a man?" And she resorted to the bottle of whisky she had started before our departure for the party. I was about to say something, but she dismissed me harshly—"Mind your own business!"—and went to her studio. Once, she had written a beautiful novel there. Since the publication of the List she just used it as a private place to drink. And I fell into despair, for it was I who was responsible.

TWO DAYS AFTER RAYMOND HAMMETT'S MURDER SERGEANT Sayers appeared in my office.

I was fairly well informed about the Hammett case by the local press, because a campus murder was newsworthy. I knew that the murderer strangled Hammett with a piece of string in his wife's studio; that his wife, Mary Mather, spent the night in her cottage at Lake Simcoe and therefore had an alibi; and that police were interrogating some suspects. The campus grapevine revealed the identity of at least one of them: Kelly, a psychology professor and notable boozer. Some colleague ratted to the cops that Kelly had recently declared, while under the influence in the faculty club, that he that he would strangle Hammett with his own hands, because he had slept with his wife. Now the sergeant told me further details.

"Listen, Miss Sayers," I interrupted the flow of eloquence of my slightly plump student. "Perhaps you should not tell me such things. They were not mentioned in the papers. Until and unless I can read about them—"

"Normally I would not pass information to you, sir," said the sergeant, who half-closed her eyes, looking at me. "But I thought that perhaps instead of that Locked Room Mystery ... which is awfully abstract anyway, isn't it? This ridiculous Uncle Abner with his 'Doomdorf Mystery'—maybe in the mid-nineteenth century they didn't know as much about ballistics as we do now. But a rifle that goes off because—" And she recounted the plot of Melville Davisson Post's classic story featuring the pious shamus Uncle Abner, in which the Good Lord Himself enters the locked room in the form of sun rays, and ignites the cartridge in the fowling piece lying in two dogwood forks against the wall, which thus becomes an instrument of His wrath. "I'd rather attempt something in the manner of 'The Mystery of Marie Roget,' if you know what I mean."

I knew what she meant, and became curious.

"So you want to puzzle out a real-life murder? Like Poe?" I looked at her, and added, "You know that he didn't succeed. In fact he botched up the case terribly. Taking a mismanaged abortion for murder!"

"I know all that," said Sayers. "You analysed the story for us. Nevertheless I'd like to try. I feel confident that I'll identify the murderer before Captain Webber does. It was me, after all, who found the most important clue. So far," she added.

Captain Webber was her boss, and clues were scarce. In the metal box which contained Professor Mather's files, one drawer had been slightly pulled out, and the folder marked

Pasternak, Mortimer was open. Obviously, somebody had been rummaging through the files, and in the *Pasternak* folder the sergeant found a piece of chipped-off nail polish. Sayers deduced that it belonged to somebody who, that Hitchcockian night in Professor Mather's house, had a rendezvous with Hammett and killed him. That was not all: from the clenched fist of the strangled playboy Sayers extracted a button, the kind they sew on tweed jackets.

Captain Webber immediately made light of the significance of the nail polish: the murderer *strangled* Hammett, and one needs quite a lot of strength to accomplish such a feat, more strength than a wearer of nail polish could be assumed to have. The conclusion wasn't quite politically correct; on the other hand, the captain praised the sergeant for her interpretation of the remaining clue: the murderer was someone clad in a tweed jacket.

I didn't tell the sergeant about the button that Sidonia had ripped off just such a garment. I was curious to see whether she would be able to sniff out the owner of a missing button.

For the time being, the captain left open the implication of the pulled-out drawer. After he'd learned from Professor Mather that she quite often forgot to close the file cabinet, and that, after her husband's death, she checked all her important papers and found none missing, the captain excluded this clue as well.

CHAPTER FOUR

How I Failed Sidonia When She Needed Me Most

IN THE COUNTRY where we had lived before, both Sidonia and I had troubles, unknown and therefore uninteresting to people in the country where we lived now. When I mentioned these troubles at a party, people did show interest, but it was about as real as my own interest in the chances of the Baltimore Orioles reaching this year's World Series, or something of that order.

And what kind of troubles did we have? I had written a novel that some higher-up in the Party didn't like, and Sidonia's father had emigrated to America without a passport, travelling on all fours and hiding in bushes all the way across the border. My peccadillo had consequences that were, all in all, bearable: On orders from the Central Committee of the Party, my novel was trashed first by literary critics, then by the police. I was demoted from my post as assistant editor-in-chief of the bi-monthly *Literature in the World* to proofreader, at a considerably reduced salary. For Sidonia the consequences of her father's departure were more serious. She performed as a singer in the state ensemble, called Daisy, which existed chiefly for the purpose of going on foreign tours. The company was an export business, and Sidonia, like all young girls in that country where foreign travel wasn't just a matter of getting a passport, yearned to visit distant parts of the world. But whenever the ensemble travelled to those parts, Sidonia, because of her daddy's misdemeanour and his current place of abode (the Bronx, N.Y.), had to stay behind and work temporarily in the ensemble's office, even though all work there ceased as soon as Daisy crossed the border.

Many people in that country held similarly inactive jobs. My lazy cousin Arnost Lustig, for instance, was a district secretary of the Socialist Party, whose negligible membership consisted chiefly of paid "secretaries" like himself. The only reason the shadow party existed was to allow the Communist Party to present the republic as having a multi-party system.

But people like my lazy cousin took such jobs with the full understanding that they would have nothing to do. Sidonia had become a singer in Daisy not out of laziness but because, for one thing, she had to support a preteen sister and a mother who was unemployable as the wife of a man soon to be an American citizen, and for another, because she wanted to see big foreign cities. Like their father, her older brother had also attempted passportless foreign travel, for which he received fifteen years and became an additional liability to Sidonia. Besides, unlike other similarly paid yet *de facto* unemployed persons, Sidonia was in danger of being fired, for being a useless employee of wrong class origin.

And so, out of sheer stupidity, I followed the advice of my lazy cousin Arnost, who had the reputation of knowing where to pull strings—his well-remunerated unemployment seemed to confirm that—and went to the Ministry of the Interior. There I asked for an interview with the comrade who was in charge of supervising Daisy. I intended to explain to him that Sidonia had exemplary proletarian origins, and that it was a mistake to accuse her of having "bourgeois roots," just because she had a father in America and a brother in a concentration camp.

EVEN BEFORE ARNOST'S DIM ADVICE, I HAD CONSIDERED doing a novel about Sidonia's life, not with literary intentions in mind, but in order to help improve her class image. I imagined the opus as a Dickensian narrative about how my wife was born in a seedy hotel during the Great Depression, because her out-of-work daddy had been evicted from the family's flat. For humorous relief, I intended to include Dickensian minor characters: her coal-miner grandfather, who lived on bacon and rum and died at forty from cirrhosis of the liver; her grandmother, a social-democratic suffragette who would escort her seven children to meetings to provide herself with a claque, etc. The Communist Party had not existed in those days, so later, in Communist Czechoslovakia, old social democrats were regarded as social-fascist. I wanted to dispel that dangerous image and restore Sidonia's credentials as a woman of the people.

All that came of that proposed novel, as with many literary intentions of mine, was a short story, and the censors banned it for lacking a Marxist approach. The tale, called "Oh, My Papa!" opened with the sentence, "My trouble is that I am of bourgeois origin. In the old days this was an advantage, but in those days I was not of bourgeois origin." The censor explained to me that according to Marxist-Leninist teachings, class origin was an unchangeable constant, and recommended the study of Engels's *The Origin of the Family*.

I received a similar lecture at the Ministry of the Interior. To the comrade who seemed to be listening to me with disgust, but was perhaps only sunk in some class-conscious gloom, I told Sidonia's life story, which I had memorized at home in minute detail, beginning with how she had not been admitted to elementary school because of malnutrition, and so on all the way to her father's arrest by the Gestapo after many years of unemployment. In short, I painted a picture for the benefit of the StB agent, in thick and most fashionable colours, using an almost socialist-realist brush. But when I paused briefly to catch my breath, the agent said, "Oh, well," opened a folder lying in front of him, and asked, "Have you finished, comrade?" "Not yet," I said, and rhymed off a few more touching details in an effort to shut him up, but the comrade ran his finger over some lines, stopped me, and asked another question. "What you've told me is all very well, but how do you explain that your wife's mother, allegedly a coal-miner's daughter, on 12 May 1954 in the state butcher shop on Karlin Street, number 37, said that the comrade president was an ass?"

There was, of course, a simple explanation: Sidonia's mother was right. But I could not possibly tell the comrade that.

Soon after my failure at the Ministry of the Interior, Sidonia's politically correct colleagues went on an interesting tour to Finland, or to Italy; she as usual was left behind to keep regular business hours in her locked office. Then, all of a sudden, Sedlacek appeared in the abandoned Daisy office for the first time. Idiot that I was, I did not connect his appearance with my recent visit to the Ministry of the Interior.

LATE THAT AFTERNOON, IN THE HALF-EMPTY CAFETERIA, I found Sergeant Sayers in a brown study. She was gazing with unfocused eyes at the television screen, which emitted bursts of disgusting mechanical laughter from time to time. I thought that she might be sad because she had not yet managed to catch the murderer of the late Hammett, and so feared she would get an F in my seminar. As usual I was off-target.

"Do you remember how Oprah looked only a month ago?" She turned to me with desperation in her eyes.

"Who?"

"Oprah."

I couldn't recall a student with that curious name, but the sergeant was pointing to the handsome black woman on the TV screen, who was prying intimate sexual details out of a couple. Once again I had been found guilty of TV illiteracy.

"Just like me, and only a month ago!" said the sergeant in tragic tones, and tears glistened in her eyes. "And I've been on a Slimfast diet for three months. Exactly like her!"

I looked at the black woman, and then at the sergeant, who got up and turned to face me. She looked the same as she had the moment she first came to my seminar, in the very same jeans, which fitted her like the skin fits an apple. It was obvious that she was a little overweight. In her mind, however, it wasn't just a little.

33

"I don't see any difference between you and that"—I glanced at the screen—"Opera."

"Oprah," she corrected me bitterly. "I know you're a kind man, but you don't have to lie to me. I know perfectly well that I look like a hippopotamus."

"Wait, Sergeant Sayers—"

"I do. When I stand between Quentin and Henderson," she said, and wiped her eyes with tissue paper. Then she made a little ball out of the tissue, and, with a virtuoso throw across the room, sank it precisely in a wastepaper basket; not for nothing was she the pivotperson of the Mississauga police-women's basketball team. She hoped the game would help her lose weight, but I didn't think it would. In the old days they called it fate, later on metabolism, nowadays DNA, and it was all the same.

"Dorothy—" I said gently, knowing that it would not alleviate her sorrow, and she, like a true policewoman, rejected my attempt at kindness.

"Never mind," she said, wiping away her tears. "We had to cross Kelly off our list of suspects."

"SIDONIA!"

I was shocked. She had just returned from her first rendezvous with Sedlacek, and told me she had agreed to give him a written report.

"Well, it was clear to me right away why he wanted to know about Julie," said Sidonia in an uncertain voice. "She keeps dating that medical student Markovic. That's why he asked me for a report. Markovic is Serbian, see? Marshall Tito's subject."

Markovic was an agreeable fellow, but he *was* Serbian. In those days it was almost like being a Jew in only slightly earlier days.

"So I thought I would help Julie. If he asks me for any more reports I'll simply tell him to kiss off," Sidonia said in the same shaky voice. I understood that tremor. Some months before they had interrogated me about a *Webster's* dictionary sent to me, at my request, by Sidonia's dad in New York. *Not* at my request, he had added an issue of *Partisan Review* that included an article about the split between Moscow and Markovic's President Tito. It had taken me three hours of walking along the Moldau River to finally calm myself.

"How in heaven's name do you expect to help her?"

"Well, I'm going to write that she is dating a Bulgarian. They don't object to those," said Sidonia. "And I'll describe her as a good comrade, which like a fool she is. And to avoid sounding untrustworthy for making her such a model person, I'll add that sometimes she is lazy and doesn't wash her hair often enough. This will throw a favourable light on her character."

Politically, she was dead on. Sedlacek appeared just when the campaign against bourgeois lookism was in full swing. My cousin Eve had been expelled from the medical school because Professor Vorel, the leading Czech Lysenkoist, smelled perfume on her during biology lab.

And that was when I failed miserably. Sidonia, after all, was only twenty-one and even more inexperienced than I was, and if I had advised her not to help Julie—or any other friend, for that matter, because such deeds of solidarity are always dangerous in the Empire of the Proletariat—she would have listened to me. Instead I approved the silly project. An asinine hope flashed through my mind, that what had not been accomplished by my short story and my expedition to the Ministry of the Interior might perhaps be accomplished by Sidonia's willingness to oblige this new Interior agent (although not exactly as he expected).

We had only a few moments to discuss the matter, because I had to leave for an indoctrination session for non-Party employees of the magazine *Literature in the World*, and during that slow hour of boredom my supernatural stupidity dawned on me by degrees. But when I returned home it was too late; Sidonia was gone. She was at that moment handing Sedlacek her report about the model comrade Juliette, who applied political correctness to shampooing her hair and chose lovers according to their nationality.

Horrified, I wondered what Sedlacek would demand next time, and what he would threaten Sidonia with if she refused to sign up for regular service. I tried to console myself with the thought that he had nothing worse to blackmail her with than a brother in camp and a father in America, and they knew about those already. As for me, they were probably aware that before Sidonia I had associated with a certain Geraldine, but only on a sexual level; I'd had no idea about her contacts with the British Embassy. Well, strictly speaking, I did have an *idea*, but to be on the safe side I never asked her for details. Besides, it had been two full years since they nabbed her, and they'd left me alone. There was also that American Oatis Press Agency, where I had gone four years before to get information about employment opportunities. But I never followed up on the information, so I was not harassed when they snatched Oatis and accused him of being the ringleader of a CIA spying network. It was now too late to include me in Oatis's or Geraldine's old conspiracies, or so I hoped, and I doubted the authorities would create a new one just for me. There was my novel, but that was common knowledge; they couldn't extort me with that.

Nevertheless, and in spite of all such rationalizations, I suffered for some time with stomach trouble. When Sedlacek failed to show up for the next meeting with Sidonia I was still dense enough to think that Sidonia's written homework, which she had submitted to him as a report on her best friend, convinced him that with stupid agents like that he wouldn't get a promotion. Later on I ascribed his lack of interest in my wife to the prayers I was pestering the Lord with in the church of St. Mary on the Snows. But it was Sidonia who noticed a little news item in the papers, headlined "Tragedy on Highway," although she saw no significance in the accident and did not connect it with herself. The story informed readers that on the Pelhrimov highway 24-year-old Milan Nespravny lost control of his Harley-Davidson, struck and killed a 12-year-old "J.N." and ran headlong into a post, later dying in the Pelhrimov hospital.

This time, like a good detective, I put two and two together: there had been no word from Sedlacek in two weeks, and at the second and final meeting with Sidonia he'd invited my wife to join him, following their next rendezvous, for an outing on his Harley-Davidson.

"But his name is Sedlacek, isn't it?" objected Sidonia. I explained that "Sedlacek" was one of the generic names used by the StB agents. I hoped I was right, and my pious wish came true: there was no word from Sedlacek, not even after two months. We were relieved, and because bad things have a tendency to be forgotten, soon we consigned the episode of Sidonia's enforced homework to oblivion.

What remained was my young marriage to a wife who was daily getting prettier. I hoped that it might be sex with me that was improving her looks, but that couldn't have been the reason. She'd had several lovers before me. I decided it must be the spiritual effect of marriage, although that was unlikely too. Sidonia was a heathen and would not go to church with me.

In the StB files, Julie's lover was given honorary Bulgarian citizenship and the case was apparently closed. Unfortunately, before he died on the Pelhrimov highway, Sedlacek had managed to also open a file on Sidonia. We knew nothing about it at that time. We learned about it forty years later from the weekly journal *Kill Kommunism!*, published by Mr. Mrkvicka.

"YOU REALLY BELIEVE THAT YOUR BOSS EVER SERIOUSLY suspected Kelly?" I asked Sayers. "Kelly is no homicidal maniac, just an alcoholic. He may be jealous, but he isn't a macho Italian bricklayer, merely an Irish professor of psychology."

"We examine every suspicion on principle," said the sergeant. "Unfortunately, Kelly had an alibi, which smashed two of our hypotheses with one blow."

"Can you be a little more precise, Sergeant Sayers?"

"At the critical time he was being unfaithful to his wife with Jennifer Brown, and she gave him an alibi."

"And?"

"Can't you see, professor? Brown was under suspicion herself."

SIDONIA AND JULIETTE WERE FRIENDS; AS THEY USED to say among girls then, bosom friends. Their alliance was, perhaps, a little strange: Sidonia was Daisy's black sheep, after all, whereas Juliette's photograph frequently appeared on the "honour board," pinned up by the political commissar Marie Sochova. But Juliette explained away her companionship with Sidonia by applying ideology: she was "influencing Sidonia in the proper direction." And Juliette did everything to deserve the honours she received. In those early days she was a true believer, and to her Sochova was something like comrade Stalin's personal representative in the Daisy ensemble. By singling Julie out for praise Sochova was preparing her for eventual membership in the Communist Party—the crowning honour.

In the end, two men destroyed Sochova's dream: Markovic and Sedlacek. Markovic because of his politically incorrect ethnic background, and Sedlacek because he was killed before Sochova could report to the higher-ups what Sidonia had falsely told him about the kosher ethnic background of Julie's current lover. Markovic refused to recant his ethnic roots, spent some time in the cooler, and was then expelled from Czechoslovakia; Julie was rejected by the Party committee of Daisy, who decided that she was not yet ready for the highest honour. In fact, Sedlacek's fateful ride on his Harley-Davidson actually saved her from joining the Party. Had he passed Sidonia's made-up report where he was supposed to pass it, Sidonia would have been guilty of damaging Julie's happy future.

As it turned out, Julie shortly afterwards made the acquaintance of a film comedian, Partyless but extremely popular among common folks, and he ruined her morally. She started shampooing her hair, began drinking under his influence, got pregnant by him, married him, stopped drinking, bore him three children and urged him to quit alcohol as well. However, the comedian lacked the biological incentives that encourage abstinence in women; he put on weight and died prematurely of cirrhosis of the liver. Juliette never became a Party member. But the fact remained that before her marriage and all its consequences, she *had* been Sidonia's bosom pal, and remained her bosom pal through all their girlish somersaults and all the turnabouts of the times. An intimacy bound them together, the sort that often occurs between young women: I cannot be sure on the point, but I suspect that immediately after I'd seduced Sidonia, she confided the news to Julie. I happened to enter a coffee house where Juliette was sitting with her popular comedian, and from the moment I appeared, she kept her eyes glued on me, and even gave me a little smile, which so irritated the comedian that he sized me up with an unfriendly glance. Julie could not have been trying to flirt with me, although bosom friends have a tendency to do just that.

No, theirs was the kind of close girlish intimacy that an outside observer might find hard to distinguish from a homo-erotic relationship, although it was nothing of the kind. The summer before I met Sidonia, the bosom pals had embarked on a walking tour through eastern Slovakia, where they collected folk songs, ditties not officially known because they contained so many four-letter words. They slept in barns, with the permission of the farmers, spending their evenings watching the stars from little barn windows, and talking almost until dawn. Then they would be awakened by a fieldhand, come to the barn to get some hay for the cattle. Those nocturnal conversations of young women bound by intimate friendship are one of the mysteries of the human race. What did the two girls talk about, night after night, from sunset till nearly daybreak for three weeks? Not quite three weeks: when their vacation was almost over they had to flee Slovakia. The fieldhand in their last barn came not in the morning but at night, and not for the purpose of getting hay for his cattle. He broke his leg in a fall from the ladder, and the bosom friends made themselves scarce before dawn.

And Sidonia, because of that true friendship, kindly wrote a false report to help Julie, and almost succeeded in sealing her friend's fate as a member of the Communist Party.

CHAPTER FIVE

How Sergeant Sayers Abandoned Her Intention to Follow in Poe's Footsteps, and Decided in Favour of Uncle Abner

T HE SITUATION HAD rich comic potential. A novelist could have made good use of it: the Crown witness being a suspect herself. Serious criminologists, however, are no lovers of comedy, and Sergeant Sayers was offended by my laughter. I immediately apologized, for I did not want my source of information to run dry. No such danger threatened, though.

"In a detective story it might be funny, even though not very," said the sergeant severely. "But we are investigating a real murder."

"You're right, and I apologize. But I had no idea that Mrs. Brown was also a suspect."

"Why, I told you!" The sergeant stopped. "Or did I?"

"You didn't." I was on the brink of advising her not to divulge any more sensitive information, but she seemed ready to tell all, and my curiosity won.

"We found a porno video among the victim's possessions. Brown is on it, with Professor Kelly."

Until recently, blackmailers usually dealt in pornographic photos, secretly obtained and in black and white only. But these old-fashioned methods had been overtaken by technological advances. It crossed my mind that blackmail by computer might soon be possible somehow, if it was not already; however, like mathematics, computer science was outside the range of my expertise.

But the comedy acquired a new dimension.

The sergeant was continuing to spill the secrets of the police investigation: "Our deduction, therefore, was that the late Hammett had blackmailed Brown, and initially we thought that she was the murderer. But Kelly gave her an alibi which was confirmed by the desk clerk at the Xanadu motel. The clerk remembered the two of them renting a room for the night in question. And Brown was with Kelly when he paid his bill in the morning." She scowled. "That gave Kelly an alibi."

She paused, and I made no comment.

"They are the only two suspects," she said gloomily after a while. "At least, for the time being."

I thought about suspects in the world where we had lived before, for whom there were no alibis, and how after the regime of onetime revolutionaries turned finkmasters had collapsed in the year of grace 1989, Sidonia flew over there to get a medal.

Then I remembered two observations made by my desperate wife, one concerning Hammett and Lorraine Henderson, and the other, after Hammett's death, concerning a button. But I did not divulge them to the sergeant.

EVEN BEFORE THAT REGIME FINALLY PERISHED, NOT with a bang but with a whimper, my wife's behaviour had become suspect among her fellow expatriates in Toronto. But she was able to shed that suspicion. Under the weight of evidence, a Mrs. Parsons (née Vrtichvostova) confessed that she was the source of a certain rumour. Mrs. Parsons' activities in the Czech community of Toronto were similar to those of her namesake in Hollywood.

"That Sidonia flies to Prague?" I asked.

"Apparently," said Jarmila Akuratova, whose main claim to fame was that she was the Czech community's prettiest married woman, "she does it every other month. She uses her Canadian passport for evening departure; in the morning she is in Prague and uses her Czechoslovak one. A black limousine is waiting for her at the air terminal, takes her to the Ministry of the Interior, she gives her report, the limousine takes her back to the Ruzyne airport, and in the afternoon she leaves for Canada. At four p.m. local time she lands in Toronto, so that she manages the whole trip in less than twenty-four hours."

"This is not hearsay? Mrs. Parsons told you personally?"

"Me personally," Jarmila nodded gleefully.

Some six years later, after the Velvet Revolution and Mr. Mrkvicka's List, I remembered Mrs. Parsons' allegations about Sidonia's trips to Absurdistan, as its citizens nicknamed their old country. Was there a connection between the gossipy Mrs. Parsons in Toronto, and Mr. Mrkvicka in Prague—for whose journalistic endeavours gossip was the main source? In his fictional biography of my wife, "Put Your Cards on the Table, Mrs. Sidonia!" there were allegations of secret flights to Prague for the purpose of handing in reports.

"Are you willing to be my witness, honey?" I asked Jarmila, who didn't mind such incorrect terms of endearment.

"Sure. I heard it directly from her. With my own ears."

Jarmila's brother was a colleague of Sidonia's brother Mirek, with whom he had spent ten years in the Jachymov uranium mines, as an inmate of the Educational Institution of the Ministry of the Interior. Like Sidonia's brother, he remained uneducated.

"C'mon, then!" I told Jarmila, and we entered the subway.

That day, the presidium of the most traitorous of all the traitorous organizations of the exiles, the Council of Free Czechoslovakia, held a meeting in Toronto. As a functionary of the pre-Communist Socialist party, Mrs. Parsons was a member. So was I, as an internationally known writer, thanks to the recent Finnish translation of my opus *A Heap of Bodies*. So Parsons (married to a chartered accountant, Lou Parsons) and I were Sister and Brother, for that was how members of the Council addressed each other.

From the rostrum, in a gloomily pathetic voice, Jarmila repeated Mrs. Parsons' story about my wife's travels, and I enjoyed observing Sister Parsons as she grew pink, then red, and finally as she began using her embroidered handkerchief in the classical gesture of wiping sweat from under her nose.

"Sisters and Brothers, that's a mistake!" she declared in desperation, and the chairman, Brother Horn, asked sternly: "What sort of mistake, Sister?"

Slowly, piece by piece, Parsons concocted a revised story. According to the amended version, it was not Mrs. Sidonia Smiricky whom she had in mind, but Mrs. Amelia Zidlicky. That was a good move on Parsons' part. Mrs. Amelia Zidlicky *did* travel to Prague: she had normalized her relationship with the Communist government, for which she'd paid a pretty penny. Maybe she even dropped in at the Ministry of the Interior, although they would hardly send a black limousine to pick her up. On the other hand, her status as a person who had paid the Communists hard currency for a Czech visa made it rather difficult to defend her political honour.

Brother Horn was a little taken aback by Parsons' confession, but then he stated that to spread such rumours about Sister Amelia Zidlicky was almost as serious as to spread them about Sister Sidonia Smiricky. Mrs. Zidlicky's husband was a Brother and a member of the presidium, in spite of his wife's good relations with the Bolshevik regime in Prague, and Brother Horn suggested that a tribunal of honour sit over the guilty Parsons. In view of his wife's unpleasant contacts with the Communist regime, Brother Zidlicky refused a tribunal of honour, and declared that his wife would be satisfied with an oral apology from Sister Parsons. So Parsons got off easily. Then Brother Horn suggested to Parsons that she should ask Sidonia's pardon as well. Sidonia sent word that the public vindication she'd received at the meeting was satisfactory.

So Mrs. Parsons got off easily for what she'd done to my wife's political reputation.

But Parsons was seething with anger. Knowing her, I was sure of that.

"I DON'T THINK THAT KIND OF ALIBI IS WORTH MUCH," I told the sergeant.

"They are both willing to swear on the Bible," Sayers said unhappily. "What can you do?"

"Miss Sayers, you, as a student of criminology"—I stopped and changed my line of thinking—"and a reader of detective stories, must know why an alibi like this is worthless!"

"I know," the sergeant said. "After they'd retired to their room, he could have climbed out of the ground-floor window, driven to Professor Mather's house, murdered Hammett, returned to the motel, and climbed back into his room, through the window. In less than an hour."

"You see!"

"Yes, I see," said Sayers. "Except that we would have to prove it."

Well, naturally. In the world where Sidonia and I lived now, suspects, as a rule, were established as guilty by means of proof, not by the application of intensive interrogational methods. Sidonia's brother had made me familiar with the Communist *terminus technicus* for smashing the kisser, and other similar persuasive techniques.

"I guess I'll start constructing a Mystery of the Locked Room again," said the sergeant, sounding depressed. "Closer, though, to real crime than Uncle Abner's theory about God."

She did, but the result was pitiful, as were Captain Webber's investigations into the problem of who'd knocked off Raymond Hammett.

THREE DAYS AFTER HER CREATIVE DECISION TO SWITCH from Marie Roget back to Abner and the Locked Room Mystery, Sayers arrived for her tutorial with hope in her eyes, and told me that her boss had a new lead in the Hammett case. Then she immediately drowned the information in confusing explanations about the monkey business of an ape trained by the murderer to lock the door after his departure from the room, and then to climb out of the now-Locked Room through the fireplace chimney.

"Unfortunately, I don't think this is an entirely original method—just a variation of the sixth, or perhaps the third, solution defined by J. D. Carr in *The Three Coffins*. You do remember, sergeant?"

She grumblingly conceded that she did.

"Although," I said pensively, "this is not the same as throwing a poisonous snake or insect into the 'hermetically sealed chamber,' as Carr prefers to call the Locked Room Mystery. It could even be original, if not for a story by the author you rejected as your model. Do you know whom I mean?"

The sergeant nodded, and it seemed to me that she blushed.

"True, the Ourang-Outang in Poe's 'Murders in the Rue Morgue' is not trained in exactly the same skills. But he is a trained simian nevertheless," I told her sadly, and she, with even more sadness in her voice, said she would probably drop my class and try to talk Professor Cunninglaw into a late admission to his course on Identification of Severed Heads. I shrugged, but at the last minute, when she had already collected her papers and was about to depart, I asked her, "Do you know what I am wondering about?"

"No," she said frankly.

"The remarkable behaviour of Raymond Hammett that night."

She thought about it, then said, "Hammett was at home that night."

"Precisely," I said. "Isn't that rather unexpected, considering that we know staying at home in the evening was never

Hammett's preference? Recall the Sherlock Holmes story we read in class two or three weeks ago, sergeant. About the watchdog that didn't bark, although the murderer had entered his master's house?"

"Hmm," mumbled the sergeant. "You mean, that's Hammett's remarkable behaviour?"

"Precisely," I said, repeating myself. "Did he use his wife's absence for what such absences are used for in farces? But this farce ended in murder and the person with whom Hammett had a rendezvous in his wife's house was, according to all indications, a man."

The sergeant opened her mouth; she was about to say something, but didn't.

CHAPTER SIX

What Hammett

Did Alone at Home,

and How I Remembered

a Conference

WHEN WE ARRIVED in prague, where Sidonia intended to sue the Ministry of the Interior, she granted an interview to the independent newspaper *Everybody's Daily*, and since her conscience was clear, she described her dealings with the StB agent truthfully. It was an error of judgement. She should have remembered that to keep silent is golden, but even after her thirty-three years of life in Absurdistan she had not learned the art of tactics. The old Czech proverb about the gold of silence was translated there into the language of the wartime German occupiers as *Maul halten und weiter dienen,* and Sidonia's knowledge of German was scanty. That's why she didn't know that she should keep her kisser shut and carry on. She explained to interviewer Piskal that she had written her report on Julie in order to dispel the clouds of suspicion that had gathered above her best friend's head because she had allowed herself to be seduced by a Yugoslav man. True, in those days the Party objected also to extramarital sex, but only on moral grounds; and since according to Sidonia's report the seducer was Bulgarian, Juliette's copulation with him did not bear any political stigma. On moral grounds, the Party could have forced Juliette only to matrimony, not to the other forms of re-education that would have threatened her had they known that her partner in immorality was a Yugoslav.

Sidonia's veracity had one agreeable consequence: after a quarter of a century of silence, the best friend wrote her a letter. Although correspondence with exiles was not as dangerous in President Husak's post-Soviet-invasion era as hanky-panky with a Titoist had been in the times of Juliette's youth, Julie was still concerned about the safety of her children, and so had not exchanged letters with Sidonia for a long time. But as soon as the interview was printed Sidonia received a missive in which her old friend, as a best friend should, gave vent to her sympathetic outrage at the impudence of the dead StB agent who'd put Sidonia on the List. From the letter Sidonia also found out, belatedly, that at the time she'd tried to help her best pal via her Ministry-of-the-Interior connection, Juliette, on the advice of her political instructor Sochova, had dumped the Yugoslav and begun bestowing her favours on a Bulgarian philosophy student. Sidonia had not known that her report, though false, had also been true, and therefore unnecessary.

The bulk of Juliette's letter was taken up by lamentations about her past: under the influence of the popular comedian, and due also to her own mental growth, she had turned into a very aggressive reactionary, and now, in utter sincerity, she apologized to Sidonia for having been such an activist in the old days, strengthening thereby the regime that, in the end, did this to her best friend. For the greater part of her guilt, however, she blamed Sochova, particularly because the political commissar had persuaded her to break with the Yugoslav. It made me wonder whether she was sorry for her ideological selection of lovers, or for the fact that she had split up with a Titoist. After all, had he married her, Markovic could have taken her to his homeland, where they had agreeably deformed the Teaching of All Teachings. It wasn't America, but neither was it a land of "hard-as-nails" socialism, as Juliette's compatriots termed their country's regime. Anyway, following the Yugoslav episode, and after a very brief relationship with the Bulgarian, she met the popular comedian; she bore him children and loved him because he was a wise man of the people, though not "the People" as defined by the Communists.

I felt ashamed about my momentary suspicion of the motivation of Julie's love affairs, and I added a heartfelt P.S. at the end of Sidonia's letter. An intensive exchange of letters ensued between the rediscovered best friends, a conversation by correspondence that saved Sidonia from falling into the abyss of despair, at a time when I was of no use to her.

SHE MIGHT WELL HAVE DESPAIRED, BECAUSE OTHER consequences of the interview in *Everybody's Daily* were not pleasant. A Doc. Dr. Adolf Hrabe, Dr. Sc., in a letter to the editor of *Kill Kommunism!*, stated unequivocally that good intentions were of absolutely no consequence: a decent person had to refuse *any kind* (italics were in the original) of countac (*sic*, but that may have been a misprint) with the criminal organization and its various subsidiaries. In his eyes, Sidonia's having stooped so low as to write a report, no matter how favourable, on Julie Tyburc made her both *de facto* and *de jure* an StB agent.

The speciality of the double doctor was history, which he taught at Charles University, and the academic degrees framing his name indicated that he himself had not avoided contact with the criminal organization: it was the Commie gang (as Doc. Dr. Hrabe, Dr. Sc. called them) that had introduced the novelty of degrees both before and after one's name. In Prague I later learned that Doc. Dr. Hrabe, Dr. Sc. had retired after the Velvet Revolution, under pressure from students, and I almost felt sorry for him. His letter to the editor was probably an attempt to turn his coat back again. My life had taught me long ago that all radicalism has three sources, and three sources only: stupidity, bad conscience, and an uncontrollable personal hatred.

I WAS SITTING WITH WENDY MCFARLANE, MY FRECKLED private spy, at the bar in the Lame Duck, engaged in a conversation that felt like some kind of *déjà vu*.

"You shouldn't drink so much," preached Wendy over the glass of bourbon that had just been set before me. Neither she nor I knew whether it was my third or fourth that afternoon; in those matters I relied on the bartender, who was accurate in his accounting and, I hoped, honest.

"I know," I answered Wendy.

"So why do you?"

"I don't know."

"But you do know. You are a prof, so how come you don't know?"

"I'm ashamed," I said. "I shouldn't give such unintelligent answers to such an intelligent student as you are."

"No, you shouldn't," said Wendy. "You're an alcoholic, just like my dad. He doesn't need it either. He, too, does not know why he is doing it, and yet he drinks like a sponge."

"Because he is an alcoholic," I closed our little exercise in logic. "It's called a *circulus vitiosus.*"

Wendy thought for a while, then said, "I know what a *circulus* is. What is *vitiosus*?"

She had taken an "Introductory Latin" course, because she intended to become a priestess in the Anglican Church. I expressed my dismay, "McFarlane! Why, last semester you took comparative linguistics!"

She did it, she'd once confessed to me, because she liked the young and extremely learned Professor McLeod. Now, ashamed of her lapse in knowledge, and since she fancied histrionics, she hit her forehead with a clenched fist. "Why, of course! A vicious circle!"

At that time, however, my increased intake wasn't the outcome of a vicious circle. Since I didn't know how to comfort the desperate Sidonia, I fell into my own well of despair. Only alcohol consoled her, and when I tried a sermon not unlike the exhortations of the future Anglican priestess, she cut me off with a cruel "Mind your own business!" I bowed my head. I was of no help to her because I offered only private assistance, motivated by love. Sidonia was being crushed by the malice of history.

At that moment, Lorraine Henderson entered the Lame Duck, and made a beeline for a table occupied by a group of members of the college football team. We both followed her with our eyes. She walked erect, to show off the perfect shape of her sportswoman's body, but the Titian creation on her head looked somewhat limp. She'd probably skipped a couple of her Vidal Sassoon sessions.

"Has she been crying?" I asked.

"Yes. Because of Hammett."

"You don't say! Why?"

Wendy looked at me contemptuously. "Didn't you just now say something about intelligent questions? Or answers?"

I suddenly remembered the holding of hands, that detail noticed by Sidonia at the departmental party. Nevertheless, I played the part of an uncomprehending fool to get more information out of her.

"So the whole college knows about it?"

"No. Only me. I was with her on the train to Montreal and she got plastered."

"She did? All by herself?"

"Well," said Wendy. "I could tell she really wanted to talk, but didn't think she should, so I bought us a couple of gin-and-tonics."

"And she ordered a second round?"

"She ordered a few more for herself. That's why she didn't notice that I had stayed with my first one."

"And she confided in you?"

"Well, yes. On our way back I had to promise not to tell anybody."

"You could have told me. Why didn't you?"

I expected she would refer to her girlish promise. I was wrong.

"Because I'm no gossip," said Wendy.

That silenced me for a moment. I quickly thought about some possible definitions of a gossip. Probably none existed. Wendy just liked to talk about the people inhabiting her rather small world. But she lacked the imagination to make anything up. So she was right: if imagination is a substantial ingredient of that human type, she was no gossip.

I said, "Why are you telling me now?"

She thought again. At least it looked like thinking. In reality she was fighting temptation. Hers was a fight similar to men's fights with the bottle in Chandler's novels. The temptation to blab, like the bottle, always wins.

"Because it doesn't matter anymore. He won't marry her now. He's dead."

"So now you're going to trumpet it all over college?" I said.

She was slightly insulted by my vulgarity.

"I never trumpet anything!"

"But you have told me."

"Well, yes," said Wendy.

"Why not the entire college?"

"Because once I've told you, I don't feel the need to tell anybody else."

At first, I was taken aback by her statement. It seemed to mean that she thought I was a gossip who would do the dirty work of trumpeting it all over the college for her. But that was a false interpretation. Wendy knew that I would keep her information to myself, and use it for strictly literary purposes. Which, of course, is not the same thing as gossip.

No, her unexpected revelation was not meant as a reflection on me. She alluded to something much more intimate, though not in a sexual sense. She elaborated on her feeling, telling me that I functioned like the tree in the Greek story of the barber who found out that the king had donkey ears. He eventually whispered the unbearable secret to a willow tree. My freckled student also informed me that, as a willow tree, I functioned well. I never made a pass at her, although she seemed to enjoy my company, and visited me in my office every day, sometimes twice. She had done that even in the old days, when doors did not have to be kept open. And she had never betrayed a more than friendly interest in me, either. Perhaps it was due to her morally laudable intention of becoming a priestess of the Anglican denomination. And, of course, I was married, and, at home, Sidonia was dying of sadness.

So Wendy told me what she had learned from Lorraine during their six-hour train journey from Toronto to Montreal. Strictly speaking, she learned it all during the initial two hours of the ride. After that, Lorraine fell asleep. On their way back to Toronto two days later she remained sober, and pressed Wendy not to repeat what she had said to anyone. Since Lorraine suspected her friend of being weak-willed, and not good at keeping secrets, she eventually produced a pocket edition of the King James Version of the Bible, and made Wendy swear on it.

So now Wendy committed perjury. I learned from her that Professor Mather's husband had promised to marry Lorraine, and that Mather wasn't pleased by his request for a divorce. One effect of women's liberation was that old bourgeois prejudices, such as the right of refusal to agree to divorce, did not survive the onslaught of ideology. With a good lawyer Hammett could disregard Mather's unwillingness to be left, and simply exchange an aging well-to-do wife for a very young and very rich one—who would also provide the lawyer. The improvements on justice also made it possible to split their property in half. My judgement of Hammett's character was that, notwithstanding the wealth of his new spouse, he would almost certainly have demanded half of Mather's worldly possessions.

"Wendy," I asked the girl who had so hopelessly lost her fight with the equivalent of Chandler's bottle, "do you know Dorothy Sayers?"

"You mean the writer or the fat policewoman?"

"I mean your very slightly overweight colleague in my seminar on the writing of detective stories," I said, and I signalled the bartender, ignoring my young friend's reproachful look. Then I moistened my lips with the poison, and continued, "As an intelligent young woman, you understand that you cannot keep this to yourself. Neither can I. You have to tell Sergeant Sayers."

"Yes, but I—" Wendy stopped short of saying what she wanted to say. It dawned on her that she couldn't use her oath on the Bible as an excuse, since she had just violated it.

"Or else *I'll* have to tell her," I said.

She gave it another moment's thought. If *I* told the sergeant, I would also have to disclose the source of my information, and that would make Wendy look like a gossip, which she felt was a slanderous imputation. To expect that the energetic sergeant would discern the nuance between a legendary barber and a real-life gossip was preposterous.

Wendy sighed. "Would you buy me a drink? I don't have enough cash on me."

I waved to the bartender, pointed to my glass and raised two fingers.

"It will be my pleasure," I said.

"Hardly a pleasure," said Wendy. "It's detrimental to one's health."

The bartender obligingly shoved two full glasses in our direction.

"But I'm barely of age," said Wendy, "and *gaudeamus igitur juvenes dum sumus.*"

Although barely of age, she was already a well-educated girl.

OUT OF DESPAIR, FACED BY THE SOPHISTRIES OF THE double-doctor and by Mr. Mrkvicka's staff writers' discovery of events in her past unknown even to her, Sidonia finally flew to Prague. Juliette wrote that the only way to disprove the accusation was to sue the Ministry of the Interior. I joined her on the flight, although in spite of all my efforts I hadn't the slightest influence on her mental state. It became so bad that sometimes, when I woke up from my own alcoholic sleep in the middle of the night, I saw light downstairs in the kitchen, and of course, Sidonia was sitting there with her bottle, staring into the darkness behind the French window.

Her old playwright friend who was now the head of state recommended his lawyer to Sidonia, and she, with all the strength of her anguish, pinned her hopes on that pleasant woman. To add to her despair, our departure from the Toronto air terminal was marred by the incident of the former political prisoner Jirousek rolling up his sleeve to show her the scars left by a burning StB cigarette. On our first day in Prague, in the Film Club, the insignificant actor Emil, Earl Konrad of Hradek, made his loud remarks about StB molls who should stay in Canada and, with the greatest possible show of ostentation, put a distance between Sidonia and himself. Sidonia went pale and ordered a double whisky. Since in those early post-Communist days they did not serve ice with the beverage, she got plastered after her second double. When Juliette arrived, all we could do was put the half-conscious Sidonia into a taxi, take her to our hotel and put her to bed.

WE DISCUSSED THE SITUATION IN THE HOTEL ROOM. Julie showed me a piece of paper on which she had noted the names of various personal friends of hers, as well as a goodly number of publicly known figures, all of whom she'd found on Mr. Mrkvicka's List. It was a remarkable group; one might say, the cream of Prague society. From the Cardinal of the Catholic Church to my old friend Ocenas, the science-fiction man, to my dear pal Lunda. In the scoundrel Nazi times that had preceded the scoundrel Communist times of our late young age, Lunda had published an illegal jazz paper called *O.K.*, pedalled secretly by bobby-soxers on bikes to all towns and villages of the Nazi protectorate of Bohemia and Moravia, where there were big amateur swing bands. Similarly distinguished men and women were listed in Mr. Mrkvicka's document, including a Tomas Tyburc—who was not, as it happened, Juliette's late husband, the popular folksy comedian of the same name. The List gave dates and places of birth, and this Tyburc was born on 08/12/1943 in Prague. Juliette's husband also saw the light of day in Prague, but on 12/08/1934.

Ignoring the slight discrepancy in dates, the authors of letters to the editor of *Kill Kommunism!* focused on the comedian, who was not just popular and folksy but also very famous. An anti-Communist with an academic degree (though only on one side of his name, not on both, like Doc. Dr. Hrabe, Dr. Sc.), Dr. Rudolf Hrouda came up with a hypothesis that, in the eyes of every believer in the authenticity and total reliability of Mr. Mrkvicka's List, metamorphosed into unshakable truth.

As I learned later, Dr. Hrouda was a regular contributor to the monthly *Crosswords and Puzzles*, and an expert on conundrums. He demonstrated how a simple shuffling of numbers in the birth date of the younger Tyburc—from 08/12/43 to 12/08/34—would produce the older Tyburc, popular comedian and husband of Juliette.

To the true believers in the authenticity of the List, his numerical magic had the power of logical proof.

Juliette asked for a public rehabilitation of her late husband, but only living suspects from the List were permitted to have their reputation cleared: the application had to be handed in personally, not by relatives or friends, not even by spouses. For some time, therefore, Julie answered every new speculation about her husband printed in *Kill Kommunism!* with a letter to the editor, until Dr. Hrouda came up with a new theory: although Mr. Mrkvicka's List was *absolutely* reliable, some *minor* errors might have crept in. By his analysis of the birth dates of the two Tyburcs he had pointed out one such minor error, but now, he said, the List was truly reliable and inviolate, except for some possible *very minor* inaccuracies. Thus was introduced a new element in the game, the search for numerical and geographical shifts, on which other investigators built other theories. In spite of all the heavy thinking, none of the researchers appeared to notice that Party members were conspicuously absent from the List, with the notable exception of expellees, who were all there, every one, with exhaustive completeness.

And on the very same day that Sidonia got plastered in the Film Club, television introduced yet another element into the melee.

WHILE SIDONIA SLEPT, JULIETTE TOLD ME ABOUT THE many attempts of the StB agents to entice the popular comedian she was married to into their nets. He reported all their tricks to his wife. Since he was an actor, he acted them out for Julie's benefit, using a naturalistic vocabulary. All episodes in the farce ended the same way: the comedian directed the agents to investigate that part of the human body which, in perhaps all Indo-European languages, is the traditional symbol for refusal.

I had known Juliette's husband very well, though not personally; he was my favourite comic actor, by far. After his untimely demise, Professor Slameny from the Theatre Institute wrote a long study of Tyburc's stage technique; he analysed the reasons for his popularity and pondered the mystery of his art. Unfortunately, I did not quite understand Slameny's essay. In my opinion, Tyburc's art was built on chatter. Mine was, perhaps, not a scholarly conclusion, and I never mentioned it to Juliette, lest I hurt her feelings. But it was a fact: Tomas Tyburc lifted chatter to the level of high art. He managed, for instance, to tell a tall tale featuring human excrement in a way that not even the proverbial nuns in a girls' finishing school would find objectionable. Show me a man who can do that, and I'll show you a Beethoven of words.

I knew that the comedian had been telling his wife the truth. However, Dr. Hrouda and others on the pages of *Kill Kommunism!* kept asking Pilate's question.

I DON'T REMEMBER WHOSE IDEA IT WAS TO SWITCH ON the TV, but as if by some diabolical miracle, a handsome blonde about thirty years of age appeared on the screen. The anchorman introduced her as the lawyer representing the Ministry of the Interior. She was asked to clarify for the viewers the issue of the numerous charges laid lately against the Ministry by persons who had been "positively lustrated"—that is, their names appeared not only on Mr. Mrkvicka's List but also on the classified lists of the Ministry. And without delay, the young woman launched into her clarifications. Because the devil had arranged it, Sidonia, who was just about to lay such a charge, woke up. I tried to switch channels but she prevented me. With eyes fixed on the screen, Sidonia began to change colour, and in no time she took on her drowned look, like Marie Roget dragged out of the Seine several days after the murder.

I soon realized that Mr. Mrkvicka, on the strength of documents skillfully leaked to him by a person or persons unknown, had assumed the *de facto* position of an official government spokesman. Although in the beginning other spokesmen had stated that Mrkvicka's List had not been screened or approved by state authorities, and therefore possessed no validity, slowly such voices fell silent and the weekly *Kill Kommunism!* turned into a *de facto* government bulletin. At least, the blonde from the Interior Ministry did not differentiate between the Ministry's files, still highly classified, and the List, accessible to anyone. And she talked about intriguing things. Almost all the lawsuits so far, she said, had been won by plaintiffs, and the Ministry had to remove their names from the List, and from their own files. The reason, the lawyer clarified, was the general lack of knowledge of the *specific* problems of the classified files. The judges were not exempt from this general insufficiency of correct understanding. Therefore the judges, suggested the lawyer, should receive special schooling.

A man like myself, who unlike the young blonde had a personal recollection of old times, could not help remembering how judges of similarly insufficient understanding had been specially schooled in the early fifties by Party secretaries about the specific problems of the show trials, such as the guilt of the defendants even if they were not guilty, because guilt was in the Party's interest, whereas the old bourgeois prejudice of proof beyond the shadow of a doubt was not in the Party's interest.

And the young lawyer went on. The lack of relevant documents, which prevented the Interior Ministry from winning more of the lawsuits, was also explained: on the one hand, misunderstanding judges refused to acknowledge the validity of photocopies of such documents; on the other, before the old regime's StB agents departed from the scene, they had destroyed considerable numbers of classified original files. This fact had not been previously known at the Ministry, but somehow became known now.

MY OWN EDENVALE COLLEGE EXPERIENCE TAUGHT ME how easily Xerox copies could be altered: on quite a few occasions I upgraded the final mark, which had already been entered in the registrar's forms, usually because the wrongly graded student was of the weaker gender and came crying to my office. The method was simple: the grade was brushed over with whitening fluid, then rewritten, and the document was submitted to the registrar in Xerox copy. On the original, such an operation was easily discernible; on the copy it left no trace.

In the end, as far as I could tell, the Gordian knot of the blonde lawyer's arguments simply meant that the courts' verdicts vindicating the plaintiffs were valid solely *de jure* but not *de facto*. The absence from the classified files of compromising documents did not *prove* that plaintiffs listed as StB informers were not informers. Sidonia began to shake all over, as the Ministry blonde, looking offended, played her final trump card.

Sidonia wailed and fell off the bed, and I couldn't believe either my eyes or my ears: Juliette swore, using the ugly four-letter words she had learned from her late husband.

ON THE DAY WHEN SERGEANT SAYERS ANNOUNCED that in the future she would no longer follow Poe but would take advice only from Uncle Abner, I drove home after dark. The highway took me up the hill where I had recently given a ride to Candace Quentin, and round the mansion of Mary Mather-Hammett. No Hollywood storm raged tonight, and the full moon shone as it had in some of the most romantic films of the late Hedy Lamarr. It occurred to me that the movies had vulgarized the charms of nature to the point where a writer who was not prepared to ignore the disdain of literary connoisseurs had to eliminate them from his repertoire of tricks, even though they came from first-hand observation and not kitschy imagination. Of course, I wasn't sure what kind of knowledge literary connoisseurs actually possessed. Maybe Chandler, my old authoritative voice, was right when he wrote that the audience and the players on the field both knew the rules of football. But these were two different kinds of knowledge.

And that night the full moon really shone, and threw a Busby Berkeley illumination on the Mather mansion, which rose towards the clouds like the Bates house in Hitchcock's perennially popular movie about the murder in the shower.

Mary Mather's residence was illuminated by the moon, and the image of that elderly colleague of mine, who like many other women before her had made an improvident marriage, appeared in my mind. Her husband, twenty years her junior, lay now in the mortuary.

Mary wasn't really old, but whenever she went out with her husband at her side, she looked like his mother. As a Yankeephile, I was impressed by her pedigree, unbroken all the way back to Cotton Mather, the stern justice made popular by Joe McCarthy and Arthur Miller. But personally I didn't like her very much. One could feel her snobbish pride in that pedigree in the way she conducted herself—with almost as much haughtiness as Emil, Earl Konrad of Hradek.

ONCE I FLEW TO CHICAGO FOR A CONFERENCE ON popular culture, and by coincidence Mary sat next to me. Two conferences were being held at the University of Chicago at the same time: one sponsored by the American Association of

Popular Culture, the other by the American Mathematical Association.

I enjoyed attending conferences; in that respect, I became a one-hundred-percent North American prof, although for me the charm of these gatherings was mainly in meeting my old compatriots, sometimes from as far away as Australia. Our reunions were richly flavoured with bourbon, without which I could no longer imagine my life. But occasionally one would hear interesting papers, and some colleagues did attend chiefly for such exceptional experiences. Their main impetus, however, was that airfare was paid by their universities, since they came to read their own papers. For rookie profs, reading refereed papers at conferences was a matter of academic life and death: papers weighed heavily at tenure meetings. For those tenured, conferences were a syndrome of booze, travel, and listening to mostly esoteric papers. But after all, professors in the same field were a brotherhood, and they weren't all like Lucky Jim, who wrote his scholarly papers for the purely pragmatic reason of not perishing.

So we flew to our conferences, Mary Mather and I, on neighbouring seats. I wasn't much inclined to start a conversation, but to sit mute for an hour and a half next to an Edenvale colleague felt impolite. When flight attendants brought our drinks, a double bourbon for me and a V-8 for Mary, I simply had to say something.

"Will you be reading a paper, Professor Mather?" I asked in a tone of nearly convincing interest.

"I shall," she answered curtly. My impression was that I need not exert myself any more. So I kept silent for a while, but eventually silence embarrassed me.

"I should ask you what your paper will be about, but I won't. I am afraid your field is a *terra incognita* for me."

Mather smiled. "Go ahead and ask. My paper will hardly be about mathematics. Even though mathematics will give it what you literature professors would call a *pointe*."

"In that case I certainly won't ask."

"You don't have to understand mathematics to comprehend the *pointe*."

"Really?" I had not expected my chat with an elderly mathematician to be fun, but suddenly a thought occurred to me.

"Really," said Mary.

"What will it be about, then?"

Mary sighed. "You may have heard about the tragic death of my dear friend Mortimer Pasternak from Cornell—?"

I nodded. As it happened, one of my old countrymen, Oskar Plawetz, taught mathematics at Cornell. He was, moreover, the husband of a very pretty woman, a former typist in Sidonia's publishing business. Oskar was the possessor of brilliant little grey cells, and also a notorious hypochondriac. He reminded me of someone, probably a literary character. In the end, due to his numerous imaginary illnesses, and despite the brilliant career that clearly lay ahead of him, his pretty wife left him. She exchanged the sickly academic for a young man, a salesman of sorts, with neither skills nor qualification and with a clearly uncertain future. Soon afterwards, the mathematician remarried. His new wife was another, equally pretty countrywoman, this one a maternal type, although in the old country she had been an operetta *soubrette*. In her purse, she carried a plastic container with many little compartments, in which she kept her husband's drugs. He took them at various hours during the day, firmly convinced that if he missed even one, he would drop dead. Proverbial prof that he was, he often forgot his pill, and so he put his wife in charge of his personal dispensary. Since his wife refused to attend his lectures, he kept the container on the rostrum, and the wife, at home, watched the clock. Whenever a pill was to be swallowed, she rang her hubbie up on his cellular phone.

Secured in this way, Oskar was shocked when his colleague Pasternak, one year his junior and without the slightest warning from his physician, suffered a fatal heart failure. He wrote me a letter about the tragedy, hoping that I would dispel his worries; which I dutifully tried to do, but, in vain.

So it happened that I knew about Mortimer Pasternak. Death had struck him in his office, where he was later discovered by another mathematician. According to the press, Pasternak was lying face-down on his desk, atop an electricity bill.

"I heard about that tragedy," I said to Mary. "A friend from Cornell mentioned it to me."

"My paper is, in fact, a sort of scholarly obituary of Mortimer Pasternak," said Mary. "Mortimer was my nephew, once removed. We grew up in Salem together, and we remained very close. Mortimer was one of the best specialists in quantum mathematics in North America. Probably the very best. The day before he died he had written me a letter ..." Mary swallowed and, for a second, remained silent. "... A very touching letter. I consider it my duty to remind the mathematical world of who Mortimer Pasternak was, and I shall quote from his letter. The dead are usually forgotten so soon."

I performed, convincingly I thought, an actor's etude of sympathy, and Mary thanked me.

"But Professor Mather," I said after a minute of silence. "You were talking about a mathematical *pointe* to your paper—"

Mather stiffened. She took her time to answer, and then she uttered almost coldly, "I'm afraid you wouldn't understand it."

"A short while ago you assured me that one doesn't have to have even an inkling of math to understand that *pointe*."

Mary had not put it in exactly those words. But the meaning was the same. She hesitated, and at that moment the flight attendant ordered us to fasten our seatbelts. We were on our final approach to O'Hare. Our conversation was interrupted by natural causes, but after buckling up I reminded Mary of my question:

"Well, what about that *pointe*?"

Mather sat silent, the aircraft landed with a big bang, and only after we received the permission to unfasten our belts, she turned to me. "I think that, before his death, Mortimer had made a big discovery. But you *most* certainly would *not* understand that."

We lined up in the aisle, and filed out through the exit corridor to the terminal. A bespectacled female student was waiting for Mary with a sign in block letters on it: PROFESSOR MARY Y. MATHER. Nobody was waiting for me. I wondered what Mather's middle name was. I couldn't think of any Puritan moniker that began with a Y.

CHAPTER SEVEN

About the Successful Math Exams, and How Sidonia Almost Died

SOON AFTER RAYMOND Hammett's murder, the exam period began. Attendance at the Lame Duck reached a point well below capacity, and quite often I was the only person present except for the bartender. The man had also been raised in the cinema—a different one, to some extent, yet we had much in common. As soon as I climbed on my favourite bar stool, I mentioned the murder, which was the unavoidable topic on campus at that time, anyway. The bartender, talking through the corner of his mouth, opined that the assassination was sex-motivated. He didn't name any names but resorted to a metaphor: the college, he said, was one huge brothel; in fact, all of Canadian society was a brothel. Hammett spent most of his time fucking, and paid for it with his life.

"You mean to say that one of our students did him in?"

"You wanna bet?"

"No. You are probably, almost certainly right. But which one?"

The barman grinned like Bogart in *Casablanca*.

"My guess is one of the following five." He lifted his thumb to begin his enumeration, but at that moment Candace Quentin entered the Lame Duck, distracting us both.

I motioned to her with my forefinger; she gave me a smile and swung up onto the bar stool. I could see that she was an expert bar-gymnast. Although I was an alcoholic, to place my behind comfortably on the North American throne was always hard work.

"What's your poison?" I asked, because, after all, I was her crime-story instructor.

"Are you buying?" the college beauty asked.

"Sure," I said. "But only what I consume myself. *You* pay for *your* drinks. That's politically correct, isn't it?"

She had no business being here. Her exam in Cooper's course was the next day, and given the Fs she had received for all her papers, one would expect to find her in the library stuffing her head with equations, or whatever was the subject of the course.

Instead, she was sitting in the empty Lame Duck, ordering a rye.

"Correct or not, professor," she said, throwing me her melting smile, "you'll have to pay. All I have on me is a dollar-fifty for a Coke."

The bartender placed a glass before Candace and, without asking, another one before me.

"Will you serve Miss Quentin on credit?" I asked. The bartender grinned.

"What a gentleman!" said the beauty with mock contempt, and finished half of her drink at one gulp.

"What are you doing here anyway, Miss Quentin?" I asked. "I know that tomorrow you are supposed to write the final exam in a subject in which I don't think you have excelled so far."

"How do you know I'm writing an exam tomorrow? And how do you know that my math is a disaster?"

"I'll be serving as your invigilator tomorrow. And the other thing is common knowledge. You're a very popular young lady around campus."

"Woman," she said, "to be PC."

Anybody could serve as an invigilator, even if they knew even less about mathematics than the college beauty. The exam lasted three hours, and we spelled one another every half-hour to keep our vigilance sharp, and prevent any consulting of unpermitted sources under the desk. We were sort of academic bailiffs.

"And thanks for the compliment," said Quentin. "I assume that tomorrow you'll look the other way when I'm perusing sources under my desk. Won't you?" Another smile, effective as *aqua regia* at dissolving obstacles. "Another rye," she said, turning her smile on the bartender.

The bartender threw a questioning look at me. I pointed my forefinger at my own chest, then, using both my forefingers, I pointed to the two glasses.

So I bought the daughter of the forty-ninth richest man in Canada a drink, and later another one.

After her third, like an attractive and agile monkey, she slid off the bar stool, and I, over my next drink, and later over yet another, pondered the meaning of her presence in the pub. Was she preparing for her exam with booze?

I didn't come up with an answer.

Then I had to go give a tutorial to Sergeant Sayers.

"I DON'T UNDERSTAND HOW THAT MECHANISM IS supposed to work," I told her.

"Well, it's a bit complicated," she said. "But not much. It's still better than the 'Doomdorf Mystery'. I mean, igniting the charge in a rifle by passing sun rays through a bottle of whisky on the table next to the victim, and focusing them on his rifle lying in two dogwood forks against the wall? Fry me for an oyster!" she quoted scornfully, this time from Erle Stanley Gardner writing as A. A. Fair, whose work she must have read out of diligence, since it wasn't discussed in my seminar.

"That's simpler than your contraption," I said.

"But it's complete nonsense. Even if the bottle did focus sun rays, it would be an elongated focus. It wouldn't generate enough temperature. Show me a rifle, sir, that could be discharged that way!"

Undoubtedly, she knew more about firearms than I did.

"I know that the Locked Room Mystery hardly ever exists in criminal practice. In its very essence it borders on absurdity. But outright nonsense is certainly impermissible," she said, and I scratched my ear. She noticed my hesitation and continued in a comforting tone, "My mechanism is not as complicated as you may think. Although it *is* very improbable, it *could* work. And, as you yourself quoted from J. D. Carr, 'There can be no such thing as any probability until the end of the story.'"

She got me there. Her mechanism wasn't, perhaps, over-complicated, but it somehow lacked simplicity. After the murderer had fulfilled his duty of providing the reader with a corpse, he attached a remote-control device to the lock, opened the door and left the room. From outside he turned the key in the lock by remote control, whereupon the device fell off as it had been programmed to do. The murderer now climbed to the roof, and through the fireplace chimney he lowered a miniature robot on a string. The robot, provided with little claws, grabbed the fallen-off remote-control device, and the constructor of all this machinery pulled everything to the roof. For the final stage of the operation I would have preferred a remotely directed device as well, but that would require a robot capable of climbing up the chimney. I didn't even suggest it to the sergeant; she might find it technically unfeasible. As she said, "There can be no such thing as any probability until the end of the story." And in the end, for all I know about such mechanisms, it *could* work.

"I find just one fault with it," I said.

The sergeant almost shouted at me: "What fault?"

"A fault I do not find in 'The Doomdorf Mystery' you mentioned."

"*What* fault?"

"Every Locked Room Mystery evokes the expectation of magic, of the impossible: the victim in a room from which the murderer simply could not, to use Poe's word, egress. And since a solution like yours is not magical, merely based on state-of-the-art electronics, the story will disappoint the reader. The end did not meet the magical expectation of the beginning."

"*I* was *disappointed* by Uncle Abner," snapped the sergeant.

"Because you didn't read carefully," I enlightened her, as I was expected to, being a prof. "A bottle that metamorphoses into a lens, and a rifle discharged by sun rays, is of course bunk. But for the attentive reader, all kinds of hints in the story, which I do not have to remind you of, make it clear that the perpetrator of *this* murder is the Good Lord himself. And to Him, nothing is impossible. Therefore, the story evokes magic not only at the beginning, but also at the end, and consequently it does not disappoint."

"So I get an F," the sergeant scowled.

"Not necessarily," I said. "Provided you tell me why Hammett was, in such an uncharacteristic way, alone at home on the night of the murder."

"Do you know the answer to that question?"

"I wouldn't ask if I knew."

"And how do you know that I know?"

"Pure deduction," I grinned at the slightly obese criminalist.

"The carrot-top, professor?"

She could deduce quite well. But she didn't need to be a detective to pull off this kind of deduction. My friendship with McFarlane was relatively well known on the campus.

"Just deduction," I said.

Of course, she knew what she knew, but she did not want to get an F. So she told me what came out after Wendy had tipped them about the affair between Hammett and Lorraine, and then she decided to swap the Locked Room for a real-life mystery once again.

DEEP IN THOUGHT I WALKED DOWN THE PATH THAT connected the two main buildings of Edenvale campus. Spring had arrived and the sun was filtering through the foliage of maple trees and warming the benches placed along the path. All were occupied by couples, except one, where an innocuous student from my seminar, Freddie Hamilton, sat alone reading a fat tome.

I asked his permission and sat down beside him. Then I looked into his book and was able to read the page heading: NORDIC SAGAS.

That was strange. The college did not offer any courses in Scandinavian languages and literatures, and the only Norwegian on our staff was a native of Decorah, Iowa, where both his grandparents had been born as well. He did not speak any Norwegian, and taught biology. Beside Freddie, on the bench, I saw a paperback with a loudly coloured jacket: Dashiell Hammett, *The Continental Op.*

I couldn't resist temptation.

"What's the absorbing book you're reading?"

He showed me the title page: *Original Old Norse Texts with English Translations.*

"Are you taking a Norwegian course on the downtown campus?"

"No, sir," said Freddie. "But I discovered something. I guess I'll write my master's thesis on the subject." He hesitated a little, but eventually said, "You may be interested. You teach that crime-story course—"

"Any connection?"

"I think there is," said Freddie with some enthusiasm. "I think that the Old Nordic sagas were the source for Dashiell Hammett's style, and his inspiration in general."

"Really? Usually it's assumed that he was influenced by the harsh realities of American big cities, and by Hemingway."

"I'm not saying he wasn't," said Freddie, as if he were already defending his M.A. thesis. "But his *main* inspiration came from the Nordic sagas."

I spent the next hour on that bench, and Freddie, quoting from *Song of Eric the Red* and from the Hammett stories featuring a detective called Continental Op, demonstrated how identical were the respective poker-faced killers of those works, and how the authors presented their bloody brutalities with an equal lack of comment or show of emotion.

He convinced me. I was quite amazed. In my courses Freddie had not impressed me as a budding scholar.

I looked at my watch. It was getting late. The sun had reached the western building of the college and I had to start for home. I got up.

Then something occurred to me. "Freddie, where were you the night Professor Mather's husband was murdered?"

"At home," said Freddie. "I know that for sure because the next day everybody at the college was talking about the murder."

"And what were you doing at home?"

"Reading."

"What?"

"*The Song of Eric the Red.* Listen, sir, you suspect *me* of this murder?" he cried enthusiastically.

I disappointed him: "I don't. But first, all that is impossible must be eliminated, as you perhaps remember from my course. Then, whatever remains must be the truth. However improbable."

I HAD ALWAYS WONDERED IF THE ACQUITTALS IN numerous detective stories really did clear the accused of all suspicion. Wasn't there a residuum of doubt left? Even in the courts mistakes do happen. But the suspects defended with the logical antics of Monsieur Poirot or Ellery Queen all turned into lilies. And so did their predecessors in the nineteenth century, whose acquittals were often based on that century's science, with its belief in somnambulism, phrenology and the strange consequences of drinking laudanum, as in the classic of classics, Wilkie Collins' *The Moonstone*. Perhaps it was just the innocence of that former time, as innocent in its way as the present time, in which students like Linda Wessely, in my course, could characterize the horrible days of my youth as "the reign of Chancellor Führer Hitler" because she thought that "Führer" was a baptismal name given to German babies.

Then came the occurrence at the faculty club. Normally, I did not take my meals there, but on that occasion we all were present. The department was giving a dinner in honour of a new colleague, who had come to Edenvale to present herself for our critical scrutiny and scored a big success. Besides being a looker, she already had two learned books to her credit, at the academically tender age of twenty-seven, in which she employed rigorous feminist scholarship to destroy the reputations of American classics, from Poe to Hemingway to Faulkner.

At dinner, the towering McMountain unexpectedly leaned towards me and said, "I read in the *Times* that your wife is on some list of police informers of the Communist regime."

I experienced a shock not unlike the ones reportedly used for treating schizophrenics. Up to that moment I had lived with a feeling of safety based on the existence of two worlds: the one where I lived with Sidonia, and the other one where I existed among my colleagues. These two worlds had never overlapped. Until now.

"Her name was spelled incorrectly," continued McMountain. "Sniriski. But they added that she was the spouse of a well-known Czech crime writer who now lives in Canada."

I had underrated American journalists. And suddenly I understood the meaning of an old expression: to be unable to produce a sound.

"Obviously, it's some Communist slander," said McMountain, as the new colleague launched into reciting a stupid poem by some nineteenth-century farmer's wife. I did not have to react, and McMountain lost interest in the subject that burned like acid in my heart. Or did he just *pretend* a loss of interest? Perhaps he didn't. I hoped he didn't. For him it was just a news item, interesting because he knew the people it concerned. Saul Bellow once wrote: "We Americans are the best-informed people in the world. Therefore we know nothing."

Or was McMountain such a considerate gentleman that he would not elaborate on the touchy subject in my presence?

Who knows? A few days later, another item flashed through newspaper pages—no, that is wrong. It did not *flash*; it stayed in the news for some time. A famous woman writer of the former German Democratic Republic had been exposed as a Stasi agent. Better-informed people in America knew Gertrude's name from many conferences, where she had gained the sympathies of left-leaning liberals, i.e., almost everyone in academe. For them, she embodied the ideal of a Communist who courageously challenged the regime, but who did not defect or join the dissidents, and was therefore not suspected of switching to reactionary views. In the world Sidonia and I lived in now only a few conservative diehards were still convinced that Gertrude was a living Communist export article who had nothing in common with people they admired, like my wife's playwright friend who was now president.

Most papers gave the news item more than just a couple of lines: some printed entire articles. Gertrude was at present the guest of a famous research institute in California, where hardly anything was ever researched, but where various Commies found asylum: Professor Gansebraten, for instance, the celebrated Kafka scholar, who had twice been almost deprived of life by Marxism in action, and yet was unable to part with it. Moreover, a Pole, Szczypinski, also a writer but living in exile, printed a long article about Gertrude in *The New Capitol*, which damaged a considerable part of her credit with progressive Americans. In great detail he enumerated her many dubious views and actions, and thus filled a broad void in American monolingual knowledge of the export lady. L'affaire Gertrude remained in the news longer than usual— two whole days—and afterwards it moved from the daily papers to journals of opinion. There I knew quite a few editors, who soon forced me into voluminous correspondence by turning to me as an expert, because of my similarly exposed wife Sidonia, on Communist finkdom. In the course of answering their queries at length, I actually *became* an expert. In spite of their kind replies to my letters, I did not know to what degree I convinced my acquaintances that my wife was innocent. The Czech principle of the shit with the supposed grain of truth in it may have spread even to these shores.

IN THE PRAGUE HOTEL ROOM, WHERE JULIETTE SWORE and the pale Sidonia fixed her half-drunken eyes on the blonde from the Interior on the TV, I felt nauseated. Not because Sidonia was on the List—that only gave me regular nightmares—but because of the phrases the blonde on the screen had used to state her case. I had naively thought that in the era of the Velvet Revolution half-truths and hypocrisy couldn't exist. It was Sidonia's friend, the playwright-now-president, who inculcated me with such notions, for he spread them through all media. The blonde, though, cured me of the illusion.

She had that beautiful detachment of men who deal in death without being in any danger of it. The millions of people who listened were suavely informed that "Over four thousand legal charges were brought against the Ministry. It is not clear to me what the plaintiffs hope to gain." She brushed a dangling lock of hair from her forehead and delivered the topper. "An entry in the register of files, or if you wish, on the List, in no way proves that the registered person behaved as an agent and performed an agent's duties. It proves only one single thing: that he or she was entered into the register of files."

She was delivering this with a poise supposedly possessed only by deities, and she was delivering it in a country where the idea of a piece of shit with a particle of alleged truth clinging to it survived all dictatorships, and now clearly reigned supreme even in the Velvet Democracy.

Juliette again used an expression from the vocabulary of her late husband. Sidonia said nothing, just crept under the blanket.

At night I heard her cry.

LIKE ME, MY HYPOCHONDRIAC CORNELL FRIEND attended the Chicago academic conference. He came with his incredibly pretty wife who was dragging her huge purse full of drugs everywhere they went. But she did not watch the clock any more. There was a technical improvement. Every now and then, the purse produced a sound somewhat like a glockenspiel, indicating that another pill was to be taken.

I took them to the cocktail lounge, and to my surprise, the hypochondriac soon became tipsy on beer. While he was on one of his trips to the men's room, Marcella explained to me why he kept ordering bottle after bottle of what I would have expected him to regard as poison.

"Oskar is firmly convinced that it's good for him. He wrote to a friend in Pilsen that he had a kidney stone —"

"Oh, God!" I said. "On top of all of this!" I pointed to the purse, which had just made a lovely sound, but Oskar was in the men's room.

"Naturally, he doesn't have a stone," said Marcella. "You would have to know him. He has no stone, just as he has no angina pectoris, diabetes, hypertension ..." she itemized her husband's ailments on her gentle fingers. "Neither does he suffer from inflammation of the urinary bladder, from colitis, from arthritis or from asthma. He only has haemorrhoids, because he sits over his papers all the time and doesn't exercise." Marcella sighed. "But his buddy from Pilsen wrote him that the guaranteed cure for kidney stones was drinking Pilsner Urquell, three litres per day at least, and he believes that as if it were scripture. This buddy is a leading specialist in diseases of the liver." It was only now that I noticed that the half-empty bottle in front of Oskar's chair was Pilsner Urquell.

The liver specialist, who spread the popular superstition of Prague guzzlers, was probably paid by the Pilsen breweries to help them promote their beverage in North America.

"But I'm glad he advised him to drink. Pilsner will do him no harm, compared to all this poison."

Marcella shook her pharmacopoeia and the little bells inside clinked like the music of the heavenly spheres. Oskar came back and I saw that the harmlessness of the beer therapy was doubtful. He approached our table with a wobbly gait, and as soon as he sat down, he overturned the half-full bottle of the recommended remedy.

To draw his attention away from the still-tolling purse, although he didn't seem to notice it, I asked him how he liked the conference.

"Very much," said Oskar. "At least one absolutely fascinating paper. That doesn't happen too often."

"You mean Mary Mather's paper?"

"Mary who?"

"The prof from our college. She read a paper on the work of Mortimer Pasternak."

"Oh, that! That was—kind of an obituary."

"Nothing out of the ordinary?" I asked. "Didn't she contribute something new?"

Oskar shook his head.

"I don't think so. But, man—" he motioned to the waiter for another Urquell, and said with enthusiasm, "that *other* guy from your college, Hooper or—"

"Cooper?"

"Cooper. He was a sensation! He proved that—" From this point on, neither Marcella nor I was able to follow him. The purse again emitted its heavenly harmony. Oskar, however, fully in the clutches of ardour, did not hear it.

Soon after the conference, the thing I did not comprehend would become known as "Cooper's theorem."

I never understood it. But on the other hand, something began to dawn on me about the murder of Hammett, Mary Mather's husband. I just wasn't quite sure what it was.

WE WERE FOUR INVIGILATORS AT THE EXAM FOR Cooper's course. I alternated with Professor Frogg, my colleague from the English department, who was in his first year of teaching and filled the intervals between bailiff duties by feverishly reading Faulkner's *As I Lay Dying*. He made numerous marginal notes, and highlighted sentences in different colours so that the pages resembled a painting by Pollock, the favourite painter of one of the other invigilators, Randy McRandall. Frogg was apparently endeavouring to find a convincing interpretation of the famous chapter consisting of a single sentence by Vardaman: *My mother is a fish*. Later, Wendy reported to me that he hadn't found it, and while lecturing on *As I Lay Dying* he skipped the fish reference. I didn't blame him.

Randy McRandall had made a name for himself one night when he sculpted a gigantic doll of stuffed garbage bags and leaned it against the wall close to the principal's window. Now he had a new toy, which he brought to the math exams. While we were sitting in the invigilators' waiting room, he put on the desk in front of him two ancient books, and above them he fastened a mechanism that looked a little like the gimmicky tool used for forging signatures on cheques, except that it was equipped with an optical device. He began to examine the pages of the books through this device, shifting, at the same time, the pointers of his plaything along the lines of print in both volumes. I grew interested. Randy permitted me to look through his lenses, and as he pushed the pointers I could easily read the slightly enlarged print. I praised his reading machine, but he explained that it was not a *reading* machine but a *collating* machine, and encouraged me to shift the pointers myself. After a while, a word appeared, slightly out of focus. The purpose of the invention revealed itself. Instead of having to tiresomely run fingers along the printed lines, while jumping constantly from one ancient book to the other, you could use the contraption to superimpose the two images so that the textual variants immediately became apparent. I had another attack of inferiority complex caused by my lack of scholarly erudition, and congratulated Randy on his gold mine. Randy, however, had no thought of profit, and in a short time, someone from computer science patented a similar apparatus.

As invigilator, Randy got so absorbed in playing with his toy that Rosemary O'Sullivan suddenly appeared, quite annoyed that she had been forced to leave the class unsupervised to remind him of his duties. She spoke to him quite unkindly, then improved her lovely mouth with scarlet lipstick and hurried away somewhere out of the building. She had almost an hour to do whatever she was intent on doing, and of course, an hour was enough to manage even a date, as Irena had told me that swell season many, many years ago, when, with Rosta, we set a trap for her in Kostelec.

The fourth invigilator was Professor Margery Allingham. She spent her off-duty time reading a book entitled *A Semiotic*

Approach to the Variants of History in the Early Years of the Greek Confederacy. Not that it would be any clearer to me than Cooper's theorem.

I had two turns as invigilator; first at the very beginning of the exam, then when more than half of the martyrdom had passed. The dictionary definition of "to invigilate" is very specific: "to keep watch over students at an examination." Something like that was attempted only by the rookie Frogg and the scholar Allingham. As Wendy told me later (she was unexpectedly successful and got a D on her exam), the two spent their thirty minutes marching up and down the aisles, trying to catch a glimpse of unpermitted under-the-desk sources, or to overhear equally forbidden verbal exchanges, whispers and other signs of life among the dead-scared examinees. I spent my turn sitting behind my elevated desk, watching the girls pretend that they were engaged in acute thinking. To show it, they put ballpoint pens into their mouths, turned their eyes towards the ceiling, massaged their foreheads, etc. It was fun.

Candace Quentin did not take any part in this pantomime. When exam papers were distributed, she took out an expensive Mont Blanc fountain pen and began writing fluently. It aroused my interest. I abandoned my usual position and set out for a walk between the desks. I stopped at Candace's, and for a while I breathed in the soft smell of her well-brushed hair and then looked at her mathematics. She was quickly covering page after page with formulas and figures, but they made about as much sense to me as those equations with two unknowns many, many years ago—when I'd given tutorials to the councillor's daughter Irena, on whom I had a crush, and the councillor caught me kissing her instead. I returned to my desk and amused myself with observing the performance in front of me.

In my second turn, Candace, with a very ostentatious movement of her arm, threw a piece of paper to her neighbour across the aisle, Geraldine Smiley. I jumped up, walked speedily to Smiley, and confiscated the missive. It had nothing to do with mathematics and read: *He is not souced* [sic] *today*. It took no effort to figure out who the unsoused person was. I looked at Candace, but this time she performed the pantomime of hard thinking with the help of the Mont Blanc pressed to her mouth.

But she was right. I had begun to limit my intake. Ever since Sidonia, in the black night of her soul, had begun spending whole days in an alcoholic haze. I quite simply got scared.

SIDONIA'S *DIES IRAE*, WHEN HER LIFE WENT SUDDENLY from happy ignorance to alcoholic despair, came when we welcomed a very pleasant visitor from Prague. Suzi Kajetanova arrived to give a concert at the community hall of St. Wenceslas Church, and we invited her to dinner at a restaurant owned by a fellow who called himself Honest Ed. His memorable Toronto establishment looks like a railway station hall, decorated with Tiffany chandeliers and enlarged photographs of movie stars, all of whom had allegedly enjoyed Honest Ed's roast beef.

In her life, Suzi excelled in three fields of endeavour. First, she was a world-class singer, but since she lived behind the Iron Curtain, the world of her fame dwindled to the lands of socialist protectorates and Cuba, where she allegedly became a mistress of Fidel Castro. I gave that gossip only slightly more credence than I had given some years earlier to the rumour, cleverly spread by the Ministry of the Interior, that Suzi had urinated on people from a balcony at the Hotel Pupp in Karlsbad during some peace festival or other. The people, naturally, were Working People. The affair resulted in a one-year ban on Suzi's public appearances and also in an article entitled "Who Takes Baths in Champagne?" which I wrote and published in Slovakia. In the complex political history of post-Stalinist Czechoslovakia, periods of thaw and frost alternated not only on the temporal but also on the geographical level; at the time when Suzi supposedly urinated on People, a thaw came to Slovakia, while Bohemia remained under heavy frost. In the article I compared the well-known champagne metaphor to socialist reality, with the result that—well, with no result. Chattering ladies went on chattering about the singing whore from Brevnov who took daily baths in the costly beverage imported from the Soviet Union, and Suzi spent her year of inactivity sitting in her tiny Brevnov apartment and listening to Willis Conover's hit parade on the Voice of America. But her affection for me increased considerably, and when the thaw moved from Slovakia to Bohemia, I published a rhymed ode to Suzi in a popular daily paper. After that I hoped she would behave towards me as pop singers proverbially behaved under such circumstances.

Well, she didn't, because her second field of excellence was marriage. I don't allude to the fact that she has been married six times, but I note that every time she married anew she was unshakably faithful to her current husband. So she never succumbed to my seductive charms, but instead a firm friendship grew between us, which continued after my marriage. Sidonia tolerated the friendship, knowing that because of Suzi's fervent religious beliefs, she had no reason to be jealous or intolerant.

The third skill that made Suzi famous was food. I don't mean just that she was fond of eating. She was also a world-class cook, just as she was a world-class singer. But of course, she liked to eat, too, and so we took her to Honest Ed's Warehouse.

We were sitting at the table with Suzi's sixth husband, an agreeable fellow, and not more than ten years Suzi's junior. He compensated for his unbecoming youth by being the type of husband who, as the saying goes, carries his wife over the threshold not only on the wedding night, and Suzi was happy. The more so because some of her former husbands had even caused her bodily harm. But she forgave them all.

Sidonia didn't just tolerate Suzi: she loved her. They were both in show business, although later on, Sidonia came to excel in my line of work rather than in Suzi's. But the same people in the Central Committee of the Party who had spread the bullshit about Suzi's behaviour on the balcony of Hotel Pupp also spread rumours about Sidonia's Prague novel—namely that *I* had written it. This happened at a time when I was under a publication ban, and in spite of my many verbal (because of the ban) protests the rumour caught on. The male-chauvinist mind, then in the majority, could not accept that a female folk singer could achieve such a literary feat.

The fifth guest at the table was Sidonia's niece Lucy, who, at the age of nineteen, had left. People from the world I lived in now would immediately ask, "Left what?" In regular grammar this verb requires an object, yet, in its specific Czech usage, like the old Negro English verb "to pass" in such phrases as "she passed" (i.e. "for white"), it doesn't need one. To put it plainly, Lucy defected. She was now twenty-seven, but she still had not lost her admiration for the idols of her teens, among whom Suzi held a prominent place. Throughout the dinner Lucy's eyes never left Suzi, and she did not dare to take part in the conversation.

Conversation, unfortunately, turned on the subject that at the time was very hot in Prague: Mr. Mrkvicka's List. Suzi, conditioned by her personal experiences with the StB, declared with absolute certainty that the List was just another Communist *Schweinerei* (she'd picked up some German from one of her previous spouses). Her present husband was of the same opinion, but specified that it was another *StB* swinery, and Suzi told him: "It's the same thing, honey." I mentioned the letter from a Prague "friend" who informed me that my dear friend Lester was also on the List, and I remarked that the presence of Lester's name made the document dubious, to say the least. Suzi knew Lester well—he had written a chapter on her in his best-selling book *From Folk to Beat*—and so she agreed with me. Sidonia, who knew Lester even better, announced that if Lester was on the List, the Holy Father himself could easily be on it. "The Holy Father is not," said Suzi, "but His Eminence the archbishop is."

And at that moment Lucy overcame her shyness, and turning to Sidonia, she blurted out, "And you're on it, too!"

I do not remember exactly what happened then. It seems to me that Suzi immediately began abusing the Communist Party and all the classics of Marxism-Leninism, her husband uttered a blasphemous curse concerning Mr. Mrkvicka, and Lucy, who realized she'd made a *faux pas*, launched into a confused story of how someone brought the List to a rehearsal of the Toronto New Czech Theatre, and asserted unconvincingly that nobody had believed the slander anyway. And I—

As I was sitting in shocked silence at Honest Ed's, the faint suspicion that had only been smouldering all these years in my subconscious mind, somewhere at the back of my cranium, suddenly burst into a bright flame of understanding. That direct red line ran from my amateur attempt to convince the Ministry agents of Sidonia's immaculate class origin to the entrance of Sedlacek, for whom, fortunately, the Director of the Universe soon afterwards prescribed an exit. Not quite soon enough; Sedlacek still managed to get Sidonia's name into the register of files. Although, as it came out in court, he had left nothing in her file but her positive evaluation of Julie, later Tyburc, the only fruit of Sidonia's cooperation with him.

I had been motivated by love; in the last analysis, however, it was I who had begun the process, so many, many years ago, that led inexorably to all the trouble.

The finkmasters, apparently, interpreted my effort to help Sidonia as Sidonia's willingness to cooperate.

SIDONIA SAID NOTHING WHEN LUCY UTTERED THE fatal remark; but for the first time since I had known her, she looked exactly like Marie Roget dragged out of the Seine.

For some time everybody tried hard to make natural colour return to Sidonia's face, but it soon became obvious that it would be impossible that night. In the end, Suzi freed us from our grave efforts to cheer up Sidonia by remembering that next day she had a concert in Waterloo and had to rise early. Then we said our goodbyes. Sidonia mustered all her remaining strength to offer Suzi a ride to her hotel, but Suzi declined the offer, giving as her reason Sidonia's three martinis that evening, which, Suzi said, made it unthinkable for her to entrust her husband's safety to Sidonia's alcoholized hands. That was merciful hypocrisy; in the old days, Sidonia and Suzi criss-crossed Prague in Sidonia's Skoda Felicie (bought with royalties from my banned novel), while both then-young women were much more under the influence than any of us were that evening at Ed's Warehouse. Suzi's husband hailed a taxi, and offered a ride to Lucy, who lived near the hotel, so that Sidonia could not object.

She drove me home, and the first night of her, and my, purgatory followed.

A COUPLE OF DAYS AFTER THE EXAMS I RAN INTO Quentin at the Lame Duck. She sat next to two young men with rings in their nostrils; one had his left ear riveted through with metal, the other displayed the same embroidery in his right. But their finery was nothing compared to that of Quentin's companion, Dewey Drake, whom I knew from my course on Major American Authors. She had *both* ears pierced many times, and moreover she carried a massive ring through her lower lip; I observed with interest as she stuffed pizza into her mouth and washed it down with red wine. The ring was an obstacle to eating, and presently a piece of salami got stuck in it. She had to remove the morsel with her fingers.

Dewey could not bear comparison with Candace, the college beauty, even though she, too, was a peach. Her looks, however, had been copied from fashion magazines and her small face displayed appropriate animation. Unlike the clever if not mathematically gifted Quentin, however, Dewey had made a name for herself as a *Playboy* centrefold. Her appearance in that magazine was only a month old, so it was still fresh in memory. Her mother saw to it that none of her acquaintances would forget by carrying the centrefold, removed from the magazine, in her purse and showing it to anyone who indicated the slightest shadow of interest. In the photograph, Dewey was dressed only in a transparent pink apron that left all interesting parts of her body, especially her genitals, clearly visible. My bourgeois prejudice prevented me from understanding why Dewey's mama was so proud, since Dewey's labia, captured in the colour photo with precision, did not seem to differ from other such organs. For that matter, her little face, too, designed after Barbie, was indistinguishable from those of other dolls.

The only one in the quartet not improved with fake gold in various orifices was Quentin. She filled her mouth with pizza in genuine student fashion, and when she caught my eyes she threw me a smile that shone with the greatest possible shininess. This time, however, I did not melt; I was angry at her because of that trick with the piece of paper in the exam room. So I put on a deadpan expression, at which Quentin turned and said something to her company; they all laughed and stared at me. Except Dewey, because another food particle was caught in her ring.

I scowled and slid down from the bar stool, with none of the bravura of a trained monkey that Candace had once displayed in this very same bar, and left the pub.

Candace either didn't care about her exams, or somebody had performed a miracle.

I WALKED OVER TO THE MAIN COLLEGE BUILDING AND entered the faculty club. As I had hoped, a company of profs was gathered there. Just as I was a daily guest at the Lame Duck, the Edenvale scholars sat daily in the much less cozy confines of the staff dining room. I asked their permission to join them, and sat down next to Cooper, who was listening to Mary Mather with concentrated attention. Employing the usual professorial humour, she related various funny happenings at a recent mathematical congress in Los Angeles, except that I kept missing the joke. Maybe I did not quite understand her English, made strange by some accent, probably characteristic of her native town of Salem.

Mather ran out of stories and a fat symbolic logician, Brendan Brindan, took over.

I asked Cooper in a low voice, almost a whisper, "How did your students do on the finals?"

He looked at me, surprised, with a scowl in his eyes. "Why are you interested?"

"I was an invigilator at your exams. I almost caught one student cheating."

"Did you? Who was he?"

I couldn't decide whether I heard interest or suspicion in his voice.

"Quentin," I said.

"What do you mean 'almost'?"

I laughed. "I'm afraid I made a fool of myself. I saw her throwing a piece of paper across the aisle. I confiscated it, and it had nothing to do with cheating."

"What was it, then?"

"It said: 'I'm finished. Are you?'"

"Hmm," said Cooper, and then gave all his attention to another chain of humorous narratives about fun at the congress. Brindan laughed at his own jokes so heartily that his belly slid out of his trouser belt; but again, I couldn't make out the humour, although Brindan spoke without any accent. I used another short pause to accost Cooper: "It surprised me."

"What did?" Cooper almost snapped.

"That Quentin was finished by the end of the second hour. The exam gave them three hours. As far as I know—a student from your course told me—she hadn't been particularly successful at integral calculus."

"Differential calculus," Cooper corrected me, without showing any interest in the identity of my informant. "She hadn't. Not much. But her exam was a straight A."

"A miracle?"

"I gave her tutorials and she never missed one. Quentin has a good head for mathematics. She's just somewhat careless, as pretty girls often are."

"What will you give her for her final mark?"

He wasn't obliged to tell me. Exam results were supposed to be classified, until students would receive them in writing. Nevertheless, he told me. "A-minus, I guess. I have to think it over."

Then he turned his attention to Brindan again.

My tutorial with Sayers was ten minutes away, so I slid out of the faculty club, in the midst of another uproar over further hilarious events in the life of North American mathematicians. On my way to my office I calculated in my head. According to college regulations, the grade received for the final exam represented thirty-five percent of the final mark.

Four term papers, fifteen percent each, added up to sixty percent. What was left was five percent for "participation in class discussions." Maybe Quentin excelled in those. But even if she got an A-plus for blabbering in class, given her four Fs for papers I couldn't figure out how she could end up with a final A-minus. Or even a B-plus. True, I always had trouble figuring out percentages, but my guesswork, although arrived at without the use of a pocket calculator, seemed about right. Or had Cooper made an error in *his* calculation? That would have to be a truly Einsteinian error.

I remembered again the tutorial, or whatever it was, behind Cooper's closed door, which ended with tears filling the eyes of the college beauty in her fashionable Gucci jacket.

No. I didn't believe Cooper had made an error. Something else was hidden in that excellent final mark.

WHEN THE ARTICLE "PUT YOUR CARDS ON THE TABLE, Mrs. Sidonia!" came out in *Kill Kommunism!*, I embarked upon an imprudent expedition to Prague. I went to see Mr. Mrkvicka.

"We, on *principle*, do not divulge the sources of our information," he told me with an air of virtue in his ruddy face, since he was quoting a Holy Principle. Until recently, he had been a fellow-travelling Marxist. Even in jail, where they had put him in 1987 for illegal sales of rock-and-roll cassettes, he made fun of the pious seminary student Olsina, imprisoned because of a letter he had sent to the president protesting the recent violation of the human rights of the Moravian Brethren divines. Mr. Mrkvicka ridiculed the Brethren's concept of non-violence, and at the same time he so persistently indoctrinated the not particularly bright dissident Vrabcak (in the clink for unapproved antiwar activity) about Trotsky that Vrabcak flattened his nose.

The initial financing for *Kill Kommunism!* came from the sales of the issue containing the classified List, which reached half a million copies. Who gave Mr. Mrkvicka the classified document he wouldn't say, since as I had learned he did not divulge the sources of his information on principle.

"In that case," I told him with amiable restraint, "I shall be forced to lay charges against you, as editor-in-chief. There are quite a few assertions in that article about my wife which are not true and make it possible for me to charge you with violation of the individual rights of a citizen."

In the old days, when my parents were young, it was called "insult to personal honour," but personal honour, at least for the time being, wasn't very hot in the new state. On the strength of that honour law, my dad had charged a certain Mr. Hrabal in 1937 with spreading rumours about my mom's bastard child, stashed away at my grandfather's. The story was partly true, except that the child was no bastard but my very pretty half-sister, whom my father eventually adopted and took to live with our family in Kostelec, where she immediately began breaking hearts with reasonable success. In spite of that, Dad won the suit; Mr. Hrabal had to print an apology in the local papers, and pay court expenses. He *had* produced a witness, who did not use the term "bastard" but confirmed that Mr. Hrabal's information was factually correct; the judge, however—Irena's daddy, the councillor—ruled that "insult to personal honour" applied even if the information was correct but the person in question wanted to keep the insulting information secret, as long as it wasn't a chargeable offence. Mom's honour was thus successfully defended and Mr. Hrabal had to pay up. He apologized, too, and twice at that: my dad thought the first apology too vague, and the councillor agreed. Nevertheless, the misdemeanour that led to his conviction achieved Mr. Hrabal's aim: to spread his truthful slanders. Mom's honour *was* discredited, for such were the times. To have a bastard was a shame, even if the bastard was a beautiful girl. Shortly afterwards, the times changed radically, the councillor was arrested by the Gestapo, both Irena and her younger sister Alena moved to their aunt's in Prague, and that was the end of my amorous efforts with both of them.

But there was, naturally, a difference: Mom indeed had had my sister out of wedlock, whereas Sidonia married me in 1958 because she loved me, not on orders from the Interior Ministry. And years later she founded our publishing firm in Canada, where she worked herself almost to death, not because the Ministry needed information on the publishing activities of exiles. She merely wanted to help Czech literature.

"And her secret trips to Prague," I continued, "using her Czechoslovak passport, as you claim in your article?"

"That came from a reliable source."

"Naturally, you will not disclose the source?"

"Naturally I won't."

"That leaves me with no option but to sue you," I said. "You state in the article quite unequivocally that my wife was an StB agent for many years, for which accusation you do not have any reliable witnesses, and you even assert that Mr. President gave her the White Lion because he himself was an StB agent. 'One StB man simply decorated another StB man.' That's an exact quote."

The self-assured Mr. Mrkvicka was unfazed, even ironical. "You missed that all assertions about your wife are presented merely as hypotheses. The article introduces her biography with the words: 'Different scenarios can be adduced about the life of Mrs. Sidonia. One, for instance, that Mrs. Sidonia is an old StB agent,' etc. The author, talking about 'different possible scenarios,' clearly hints that his is only one of the possible versions, and in no way does he claim that it is correct."

The councillor who many years ago had fined Mr. Hrabal for slander was long dead. They cut off his head with the Pankrac Gestapo guillotine. To be an StB agent wasn't a punishable offence, only shame, and according to Mr. Mrkvicka, I couldn't sue him, regardless of whether his pronouncements about Sidonia were true or false. The councillor had been the kind of judge who, shortly after his death and after another radical change in politics, acquired the sobriquet "bourgeois." Mr. Mrkvicka would not have won his case with him. But I had my doubts whether the post-Communist judges were in any way bourgeois.

"All right," I said. "But you claim that for my wife's secret trips to Prague you have a reliable witness."

"Source, not witness," he corrected me. "Let's be exact."

"O.K., source," I said. "You don't have to disclose it to me here. But since your accusation is serious, at the court you will have"—I was unable to speak without irony—"to put your cards on the table."

"You think so? I don't."

"We'll see." I got up and without saying goodbye I left the offices of the weekly *Kill Kommunism!*

As I was leaving the house, I almost ran into my Toronto Sister Mrs. Parsons in the hallway. She pretended not to see me, although usually she had eyes like the proverbial bird of prey. But I had no wish to engage the lady in conversation. The words I had had with Mr. Mrkvicka that day were quite enough for me.

CHAPTER EIGHT

Sayers Betrays an Official Secret, and Sidonia Receives an Honorary Degree

ON MY WAY TO MY TUTORIAL with the sergeant I thought about my two worlds, the one Sidonia and I lived in now and the other we had lived in before and in which we were now half living again; how the two worlds almost overlapped, but in the end didn't. McMountain had found a news item in his newspaper that blew in a wind from the old world, but Faulkner's beautiful sentence did not apply to Edenvale College: *"Through the bloody September twilight ... it had gone like a fire in dry grass—the rumor, the story, whatever it was."* Either McMountain was a gentleman or the affair didn't interest him. Most likely, as a North American, he had an almost instinctive distrust for any naming of names, and so he fully sided with Sidonia although he didn't talk about it. Perhaps nobody else at the college noted the story in the *New York Times*, or maybe they were all similarly conditioned.

And so one day Sidonia received a letter from the president of Edenvale College's parent university. She opened it with apprehension, and then sat down. The president was telling her that the university, in view of her many years of selfless cultural labours for the Czech community in Canada, had decided to bestow an honorary doctorate on her.

I, too, received an honorary degree. For my detective stories, I guess. Most professors suffer from the secret vice of reading such stuff, even if in their courses they lecture on Elizabethan poetry and Shakespeare. But the bard, too, in a sense, wrote crime stories. Dickens, then? Well, Boz was the author of several thrillers. Mark Twain? What about *Pudd'nhead Wilson*, not to mention *Tom Sawyer, Detective*? Faulkner? Who concocted *Knight's Gambit* and *Intruder in the Dust*? For a while it seemed to me that everybody in English and American literature wrote crime fiction, except perhaps Victorian female writers. However, that deficiency was corrected by British ladies in the twentieth century and by Yankee women soon after Poe.

SHORTLY AFTER SIDONIA HAD LEARNED THAT SHE WAS on the List, Cleopatra and her cameraman appeared in Toronto, and moved in with us. They came to shoot a documentary about Sidonia and me and our efforts in publishing banned Czechoslovak literature. Cleopatra was a young woman whose rich black hair looked almost like an Afro wig. She was a member of the new entrepreneurial class that emerged in Czechoslovakia after the crack-up of the old regime, without anybody expecting that there would be so many of them so soon. She owned a production company and specialized in documentaries which she sold to private television stations, unexpectedly also numerous. Her cameraman was a taciturn young man, who would leave our house soon after daybreak and with his video camera fish for Toronto atmosphere. He must have been a better than average craftsman, because the city over the lake shone on the screen with unblemished beauty, exactly as it appeared to me on my daily rides home from Edenvale College.

With me, Cleopatra had credit on account of her husband, a first-class jazz trombonist, a little too modern for my reactionary taste in music but still a member of the jazz brotherhood. She gained Sidonia's favour even more easily: at that time, Sidonia was grateful for every gentle touch on her soul, and Cleopatra was not stingy with kindness, especially in the company of a bottle of whisky. Both Cleopatra and Sidonia were alcoholics; although Cleopatra's reasons, as far as I could tell, were not as good as Sidonia's. But we know next to nothing about the reasons of our fellow human beings. The tragedy of our lives, as Jean Renoir said, is that everyone has his reasons.

When Sidonia's day of glory dawned, Cleopatra and her cameraman followed us to Convocation Hall, on the old university campus downtown. There they dressed Sidonia in an academic gown, put a doctor's mortarboard on her fresh coiffure, and entrusted me with the privilege of placing the cape around her shoulders.

We walked in the procession of my gowned colleagues, the huge McMountain in front of me, with Cooper beside him, behind us Rosemary O'Sullivan who turned her mortarboard around because it became her better that way. Mary

Mather-Hammett wore a black sash over her costume, perhaps in mourning for her late husband or her dead cousin Mortimer Pasternak. There were many different gowns in the procession, mostly borrowed from the university and distributed according to size or, in the case of women, according to elegance. Under the gowns, shoes, boots and pumps of different colours showed, some with high heels; Professor Schornstein, in an opulent gold-and-red cape, stalked in Adidas running shoes.

The academics were expected to appear in gowns of their various *almae matres*, but McMountain couldn't remember the uniform of the University of Montana in Helena, which had bestowed his degree on him. On the occasion of *his* doctorate, the procession probably also resembled a carnival, like the one Sidonia and I walked in now. The cameraman was shooting his documentary, the music of the university brass ensemble sounded from somewhere, and at the head of the procession the beadle was carrying a hundred-and-fifty-year-old mace; measured by the age of Canada, a very ancient symbolic object.

Sidonia, at my side, was trembling with stage fright, which, in combination with her other purgatory, threatened to overpower her completely; I thought she might faint. My wife never acquired a university education, not from stupidity, since she was quite clever, but because she had been assigned the class origin that, on my expedition to the Ministry of the Interior, I had tried to correct. The acceptance of the honorary degree included the duty to give a short address for the benefit of the assembled professors and students, whom the president, immediately after Sidonia's speech, was to award degrees on the basis of knowledge, not community service. Dread of that ordeal precipitated Sidonia's near-cataleptic state. She walked at my side like Frankenstein's bride, her face coloured appropriately. But as often happens with people who (in the Czech student slang of my youth) are hollow like a bamboo stick, but have filled that academic hollowness with novel-like experience, Sidonia, in her much-too-large cap and gown, stepped up to the lectern, and in a clear, unshaking voice, speaking a kind of English I had never heard from her lips before, delivered a beautiful profession of love for Canada. "Canada," she said, "is my stepmother; my real mother is Czechoslovakia. Sometimes, however, a stepmother is much kinder than the real mother." She left nobody in doubt that this was her case. And in my inner sight I saw again the film of her life, and realized that the List was only the last, climactic chapter in the Dickensian novel of her existence. At its beginning was Sidonia's birth in a seedy hotel. Next the family was moved out of their flat for not paying the rent; then came the denial of enrolment in the first form of an elementary school because the child Sidonia was badly undernourished. Later on, when her father was arrested and sent to the camps, the family was moved—in the name of the Working Class—out of the beautiful apartment that Sidonia's dad had acquired after the war into a smelly mini-burrow in Karlin. When once I had to use the john in that awful place it gave me chronic nightmares. I remembered our first date, when she almost froze to death because she and her sisters had only one sweater among them, and that afternoon it was another sister's turn. And so on: how the agent at the Interior Ministry, after I had finished my exposé, read from Sidonia's mother's file the fink's report on the insult she had committed against the head of state in the Karlin butcher shop. Or perhaps how she had committed blasphemy, if not sacrilege. Yes, the List was just one, even though the climactic, chapter of a typical life in our century in our old country messed up by history twice within my lifetime, three times in the seventy years allotted by the Lord to my father.

Many colleagues asked Sidonia for the text of her beautiful speech, and Professor Schornstein printed it in the college newspaper.

The two worlds did not overlap, after all.

And that evening Sidonia, happy because of her success, and in a mood made glorious by firewater, granted Cleopatra an on-camera interview. In it, she repeated what, some time ago, she had told the reporter from *Everybody's Daily*: the story of Sedlacek and the report on Juliette, which was designed to save her friend from political harassment, and ironically caused the political harassment of Sidonia herself, even though, at the very beginning, it was I who brought it all about. In an expertly shot close-up, the effects of the firewater were clearly discernible on Sidonia's face.

I realized the detrimental consequences of that close-up only later, and in a film different from the one Cleopatra had shot when she was a visitor in our home.

WE WERE SITTING IN MY OFFICE, AND SERGEANT SAYERS was reporting to me on the contents of Lorraine Henderson's testimony to Captain Webber.

The evening he had intended to enjoy in Lorraine Henderson's bed, at the Mountain Breeze Motel, Hammett spent instead in the house of his wife Mary Mather, guarding the phone. He explained to Lorraine that his wife was expecting an important call. Mary was working on some scholarly book in her cottage on Lake Simcoe, and urged her husband to stay at home until the expected call came through. Lorraine phoned Hammett from the Mountain Breeze, ready for lovemaking, and he assured her that as soon as he heard from the unknown caller he would leave for the motel. That was at a quarter to nine p.m., and Hammett begged Lorraine for half an hour of patience; according to Mary Mather, the caller was to ring about nine.

"She doesn't have a phone at her cottage?"

"She does," said the sergeant. "Maybe she didn't want to give her number to the caller. She stayed at the cottage in order to concentrate on her work."

"Who was the expected caller?"

The sergeant shrugged her shoulders. "Maybe there wasn't one. Mather denies having asked her late husband to guard the phone. She says she was not expecting any call that evening."

"Why was Hammett at home, then, instead of at the Mountain Breeze Motel?"

She threw me a look of contempt. I felt she was losing the respect she had had for me when I'd been explaining the magical effect of a well-constructed Locked Room Mystery.

"Either Mather lies, professor, or Hammett was kept at home by something else. In the latter case, since Brown has an alibi, it was probably some other woman. Still unknown."

I grinned. "You mean the peeled-off piece of nail polish?"

The sergeant again shrugged her shoulders.

"And the unknown lady bumped him off?"

"No," said the sergeant. "You forget the button in his closed fist. The lady could have arrived when he was already bumped off."

I gave it a second's thought. "Hammett may have been a stud, but is it logical, sergeant, that he would risk that much? He had a chance to marry into the family of the twenty-seventh richest man in Canada—"

"Precisely," said Sayers. "We know from Henderson that he wanted to divorce Mather but that she vetoed the idea. Which means that as far as the phone call is concerned, she probably lied."

"If she did, how come Hammett would fabricate the tale of the phone call to Henderson?"

"He may have needed some more time to spend with the unknown visitor."

"And if Mather didn't lie?"

"She could have lied. She may have ordered Hammett to stay at home under some other pretext."

"Then why would Hammett invent the telephone story?"

The sergeant shrugged again.

I gave the matter some more thought.

"Can you imagine Hammett obeying his wife when the marriage, for all practical purposes, did not exist any more? When all that was left of it was just her hatred for him?"

"But *he* may not have hated *her*," said the sergeant. "He just wanted a divorce, so that he could make a better match."

"But she *hated his guts*. A middle-aged woman who manages to marry a man ten years her junior—"

"You think in stereotypes," the sergeant admonished me.

"Is it possible to think otherwise when dealing with motives for murder?"

She didn't answer.

"What was bothering her was, perhaps, that she would lose not only her husband, but also half her property."

"Hammett didn't care about her property. He stood to gain far more with his new marriage. Also, the divorce court isn't that simple," said Sayers.

"So let's stay with jealousy, which culminated in bottomless hatred."

Now the sergeant grinned. "And the tweed jacket button, sir? Besides, Mather has an alibi, confirmed by her neighbours. They dined with her in her cottage, and then played bridge until midnight. Hammett was murdered about nine p.m." She seemed elated. She thought she had triumphed over me in a duel of logic.

I grinned for the third time. "I'm sure you're familiar with the concept of the gun for hire, sergeant."

She opened her mouth as if we were in a novel, and didn't emit a sound.

"Well, all right. Back to college business. Show me what you have written," I ordered her.

She handed me three sheets of paper covered with print-out. I read them, and then in a duel of logic I tore her arguments to pieces.

NEXT SUNDAY SIDONIA WASHED THE CAR. NOT THAT it was dirty: she just needed some distraction, hoping it would take her thoughts to more joyful things. Naturally, thoughts are not pets that rub against the master's leg even when he is holding a butcher knife, and there had never been much joy in Sidonia's life; especially not lately. That Sunday, though, she was lucky.

She came to my study with something tiny and pink on a kleenex.

"If you were not in the habit of giving rides to all sorts of females from your college, I would say, 'Look, a clue!'" she said. "Whom have you given a lift lately?"

I saw she was forcing herself into a light-hearted tone, the same she had used before the List, in the rare times of happiness. It was a camouflage. But I was glad. We could, at least, have a conversation on a subject other than what we talked about at night.

"A clue about what?" I asked.

"That murder in the Unlocked Room. According to your sergeant student they found a piece of hardened nail polish exactly like this one in Mather's house." About Hammett's murder I kept no secrets from Sidonia.

She prompted me, "C'mon! How many females did you drive home in the last couple of days?"

"Wait," I said and began counting on my fingers, although, naturally, I was no cabbie serving the lasses of Edenvale College. I just didn't want to spoil the game, and Sidonia's cheerful mood. "Wait," I said, and held up my fingers. "Lorraine Henderson, Sergeant Sayers, Wendy McFarlane, Candace Quentin, Professor Ann Kate Boleyn, Dewey Drake—"

Sidonia interrupted me. "That's the *Playboy* centrefold? The one with the ring in her nose?"

"In her lower lip," I said. "And through her nipples."

"Don't kid me! How do you know?"

"One can see them through her T-shirt. And Wendy McFarlane told me."

"McFarlane doesn't polish her nails. And Drake uses blue polish," said my attentive wife. "So it must be either Henderson or Quentin. Your college women's libber doesn't use nail polish either."

"Sometimes she does. It depends on the party line."

In this way we chatted, and for the moment Sidonia seemed untroubled. I named five more possible owners of the peeled-off polish, two of whom didn't even exist, and Sidonia permitted me to fool her. But, perhaps, for a while she thought of things that didn't give her pain.

HER DARKER THOUGHTS, HOWEVER, RETURNED, AND kept returning to that other thing, by day and particularly by night, until the day of her trial in Prague. The court was to decide whether her charge of having been falsely registered by the Communist Ministry of the Interior was valid or not. The lawyer who had been recommended to Sidonia by her old friend, the playwright-now-president, was a professional embodiment of unwavering optimism, but Sidonia was far from sanguine about the outcome. Her uncertainty originated not in guilt, for she wasn't guilty, but from the bad experiences she shared with all those who lived in that state; Sidonia's were just more extensive than, for instance, mine. She was afraid some condemning "proof" would emerge at the trial, false but hard to refute, because unlike the easily provable alibi in a murder case, the suspicion that had fallen on her was hardly disprovable by criminological technique. Before he left this world, Sedlacek could have written for the file whatever his fancy chose to invent, and for such an action there were no witnesses. Not even the kind called, in the country where we now lived, "character witnesses," who, on the basis of the suspect's character, asserted that he or she was incapable of committing the crime under investigation. According to the List, which had metamorphosed into a *de facto* government bulletin, and which parliament deputies frequently consulted, even the cardinal and archbishop of Prague had committed the crime in question. Why not Sidonia, a former singer of folk songs?

And there was another source of uncertainty. The argument of Doc. Dr. Adolf Hrabe, Dr. Sc., retired in the meantime under pressure from students at the university and established in the private sector, was taken over by a Mr. Skrzkrk, whose vowelless name the lawyer and I couldn't agree was real or a *nom de plume.* He repeated Hrabe's maxim that a decent person would refuse any approaches by the criminal organization and its cutthroat subsidiaries. Sidonia's statement that she'd just wanted to help her friend Skrzkrk likewise called utterly absurd. He didn't explain why, but his letter prompted three other men into action. They all described how, unlike Sidonia, they resisted coercion from the StB, and refused any form of collaboration. The agents, in all three cases, used torture; one coercee even had his arm broken.

As I read the heroic stories from the distant fifties, I realized that here again, any deduction and application of criminological technique was ineffective. To make the three men confess they had made their tales up would require torture harsher than the mere breaking of limbs, which they had already resisted. The present justice system did not use torture.

ALCOHOL PLAYED AN EVER-INCREASING ROLE IN Sidonia's life. Not just red wine as when she had been a singer in Prague, but hard Anglo-Saxon liquor. She began invigorating herself with it early in the morning on the day of her court appearance, and I was afraid she would be unable to say a word. Fortunately, the miracle of the honorary doctorate speech repeated itself. Sidonia drew energy from some hidden spiritual reserve, or perhaps from booze. As if Sidonia's prior imbibing wasn't enough, Cleopatra brought a flask of rum in a brown paper bag to the court, and Sidonia took several hearty swigs before her name was called. Besides the rum, Cleopatra took out, from another paper bag, a video of her new documentary, which she said would interest Sidonia. It wasn't the film shot the previous summer in Toronto. We had already seen ourselves in that one, repeating on camera the familiar facts of the interview Sidonia had granted to the *Everybody's Daily* reporter. In the second documentary Cleopatra had used footage of us talking on the shores of Lake Ontario and in our Toronto house.

WE WAITED, A TINY GROUP: SIDONIA, MYSELF, SIDONIA'S brother Mirek, and Juliette, all three called as witnesses, and Cleopatra with my old friend Lester. He came as moral support; Cleopatra wanted to shoot us all waiting, but they didn't let her.

I remembered a summer night back in the Husak era in the eighties when Lester was visiting us in Toronto and Sidonia suffered a textbook case of nervous breakdown. At dinner, I made a stupid joke concerning her culinary art, and she was touchy about her cooking. She got up from the table, left the house and drove into the night. Too late, I regretted my stupidity, and at that time I had not yet been forced to ponder other and more profound stupidities of my life, since there was no List. I waited for about fifteen minutes, then I phoned her office. It was eight p.m. Nobody picked up the call. I phoned for a taxi and we drove to Sidonia's office with Lester. I unlocked the door, and we entered the building and climbed to the third floor, where Sidonia had her only luxury: a beautiful office, full of light, equipped with a stereo, a dozen Edith Piaf LPs, and a cage containing two cockatiels, Titus and Josie.

Sidonia was lying on the floor, wrapped in a blanket from the office sofa where she sometimes dozed off when her strength, heavily exploited toting crates full of books and fuelled by red wine, abandoned her. As we entered the room, Titus whistled the first three bars of the folk song "Run, Kate, Run!" which Sidonia had taught him, and continued with his own improvisation, for his parroting skills were good only for the three bars.

I took Sidonia's hand, but she jerked it away from me. Then Lester started humming into her ear, and we took turns trying to comfort her. It took us three hours. We kept repeating the same arguments, because what else was there to say? That people loved her, that she was doing great things to save endangered Czech literature. We had not known, then, how well Czech literature would fare later on. I felt like that talkative TV woman with the face of a country bumpkin on the Buffalo public television station, pressing viewers with incessant chatter into sending dough in exchange for a coffee cup with the station's logo.

It was eleven-thirty p.m. when Sidonia at last unwrapped herself from the blanket and let us take her home, in her car, driven by Lester. When, after the appearance of the List, I was at my wits' end, I hoped that Lester had included this nocturnal scene in his report. But I knew that Lester reported only to his boss in the music publishing house, who sent him on these business trips all over Europe, and in these communiqués he described only unobjectionable meetings with representatives of music agencies, not clandestine reunions with exiles.

Lester's Toronto trip, however, was an exception: it wasn't a business trip. It was a fruit of the decline of faith in the Teaching of all Teachings even in the highest echelons of the Party government, and of the conspiracy I myself had organized. I had sent letters to various friends in Canadian and American universities and I told them the truth: Lester, Czechoslovakia's foremost jazz historian, had never visited the land of jazz. It was an old, oft-repeated story about the specialists of various branches of culture in the land where I had lived once with Sidonia, who never in their lives were permitted to travel to international conferences, because they were not Party members. Now, at long last (I said in my letters), Lester hoped to visit the country of the beautiful music he had been writing about since the days of the Nazi occupation. He offered lectures on Czech, Soviet and East European jazz, but also on jazz in Western Europe, and given these financially strained times, he did not expect honoraria, just an invitation. Invitations from scholarly institutions were a *conditio sine qua non* of such journeys. Only if he received one would he be permitted to travel.

Permission was granted, more because of the above-mentioned decline of Party vigilance than on account of the invitations, of which he received many. I was surprised: colleagues, friends and mere acquaintances, Czech, Canadian and American, they all without exception sent Lester heartfelt letters of invitation on official letterheads of their universities, and all offered to pay his airfare. Three universities even furnished a small fee.

That was how Lester, for the first time in his life, came to America. He saw it almost whole, from windows of jets, and he was also a witness to the nocturnal trouble with Sidonia. It wasn't—by far—the first nocturnal trouble caused by overwork, but only I knew about the many previous nights of exhaustion. Lester, however, would be able to corroborate the credibility of my eventual testimony. But it was testimony the court would reject as irrelevant to Sidonia's crime.

And Lester himself, after the publication of the List, became the target for various hypotheses in Mr. Mrkvicka's weekly and elsewhere. In all of them, fact and imagination were mixed in about the same proportion as in the article "Put Your Cards on the Table, Mrs. Sidonia!"

I WENT TO THE LAME DUCK, THIS TIME NOT PRIMARILY for whisky. The pub didn't disappoint me. In the centre of the room, a crowd was assembled around some spectacle, and Candace Quentin was with them. I approached the little company, and over Candace's shoulder I saw Dewey Drake, only from her breasts up, because from her breasts down I saw only the back of Freddie Hamilton, who was examining something at close range on the lower parts of the girl's body.

At first a thought flashed through my mind that Dewey was demonstrating what the entire college had already seen in the *Playboy* centrefold, but it was something even more interesting. When Freddie Hamilton moved aside I got a full view of Dewey, her T-shirt rolled up to her breasts, displaying a tattoo on her belly, apparently brand-new: it depicted a slim female nude with a biblical inscription: *All these things will I give thee ...* I felt a little shock over the blasphemy, but then I saw Wayne Hloupee in the group and I heard him say, "Charley Lim did this, didn't he? In Etobicoke?"

Dewey nodded.

"He uses the same pattern over and over," said Wayne. "Look here!"

He rolled up his T-shirt, with the inscription: *Kiss me—I'm NOT a Bohemian!*, and a big belly appeared. It, too, bore a tattoo of a nude woman, but she was fat and strangely shapeless. The assembled students silently looked at the ugly thing and Wayne addressed Dewey in a tone of apology. "When Charlie made her, she was exactly like yours."

"You don't scare me," Dewey said. "I don't stuff myself with junk food like you. You were half your present size when we were freshmen. I'm in no danger of getting fat. I'm on a Hollywood diet."

"What if you get pregnant?" Wayne grinned. "Will you show her to us then?"

"Why not?" said Dewey. "Pregnancy is only temporary. After I give birth, I'll return to normal, and so will she." And Dewey laid her fingers on the blue contours of the slim beauty on her skin.

"Miss Quentin," I whispered to the girl standing in front of me. "Can I buy you a drink?"

My intervention created interest. In a stage whisper Wendy said, "Anybody got Professor Boleyn's phone number?"

Candace ignored the upheaval and gave me the sort of smile that had caused better men than I to disintegrate.

But not today.

Sitting at the bar, she asked me, "To what do I owe your interest, sir?"

The bartender placed two bourbons before us.

"To how splendidly you did in the exam which I invigilated," I said. "I enjoyed the invigilating. I just regret that I didn't catch you cheating."

"Are you angry with me?"

"It was just a student joke."

"I once did something similar to Professor McMountain, and he was angry."

"McMountain doesn't drink."

"The reference was not to drinking." It seemed to me that Quentin, in spite of her ostentatious sophistication, blushed a little.

"I see," I said. "McMountain is allergic to fat jokes." I paused. "Nowadays such pranks are also dangerous. You heard the classic stage whisper of Miss McFarlane? And all I did was invite you to have an innocent drink of whisky with me. And you are over eighteen."

"Wendy is a joker."

"Joker or not … To your success in mathematical science!" I raised my glass and Candace clinked hers with mine. Then she looked at me with her very intelligent eyes. I signalled the bartender and when he took action I raised another glass: "And to your success with the study of law! There is no obstacle in your way any more. The final mark from Cooper's course will undoubtedly be excellent."

She examined me. I couldn't fool those eyes. And I didn't want to. Nevertheless, she took the wind out of my sails when she said, "Even though I got Fs for all my papers in Professor Cooper's course?"

"You must have made a great impression on colleague Cooper."

"You know how to count, sir. You know that the final exam counts for only thirty-five percent. Even if I get a hundred on the exam, my final mark won't be in any way remarkable."

I kept silent, looking into the intelligent eyes opposite me. Why did she take the wind out of my sails? I felt as if she served me the ball close to the net to score a point. After a very long time, I whispered into her ear, "I won't tell on you." Then I nodded to the bartender.

After an even longer time, she asked, "Exactly what will you not tell on me?"

"You can easily guess. I saw you as you were closing Cooper's door."

"Oh, that." Another pause, not as long as the previous one. She seemed to relax. "But you won't tell on me, sir?"

"I give you my word."

She raised the glass to her lips. Before she could sip the beverage, I put my finger on the little nail of her pinkie. The polish was a strange colour, almost like copper.

"You've got a new nail polish. I've never seen it on you."

Her eyes examined me again. Then she spread all her five fingers for me to look at.

"Does it meet with your approval, sir?"

"It's prettier than the one you used the night I drove you from Cresthill to your dormitory. Do you remember?"

"You do notice things!"

I laughed. "Not me. My wife, Miss Quentin." And I said goodbye, citing my tutorial duties as an excuse. At the door I turned. Her eyes followed me, full of the searching look of a person whose conscience is not lily-white.

CHAPTER NINE

Cleopatra's Film,

and What Oskar

Told Me

THE MINISTRY of the interior was represented by its own lawyer, and he gave Sidonia's folder to the judge. I felt relieved when it was established that the file contained only one yellowed page: her ancient effort to get her best friend out of possible political distress. It seemed Sedlacek had not manufactured any evidence that would now be impossible to explain away. The presumption of innocence, once condemned by the Party government as bourgeois, had regained some validity, and so had its logical sequel, namely that it was the duty of the court to prove guilt. But a cleverly formulated forgery would still have hanged Sidonia. For how, in the name of God, could she have disproved it?

All of a sudden, I realized that the court proceedings were really upside down, or maybe inside out. Had her file revealed anything more incriminating, Sidonia would have changed from plaintiff to defendant. A strange situation: a single forgery, put together decades before by an StB agent craving bonuses or advancement, would have been enough. Most such agents were either incommunicado nowadays, or dead, and there were hardly any witnesses for little events that had happened forty years ago.

AND AT NIGHT IN TORONTO, ON MANY NIGHTS, SIDONIA, in a desperate voice, would repeat to me that she would never get rid of the dreadful suspicion; that it was like being hit by poisonous spittle which, no matter how quickly one rubs it off one's cheek, penetrates instantly through the capillaries into the microstructure of the skin, and remains there as an invisible but universally known mark of Cain.

On those Toronto nights I would comfort her, "No, Sidonia, the court will cleanse you," but she only shook her head. And then I brought out the argument always used in those old times by kind people in the country where we had once lived: that folks took such things with a grain of salt, and besides, it would soon be forgotten. Forgetting, however, was no comfort for Sidonia. She was a sort of celebrity; emigré female readers loved her; certainly those who loved her were more numerous than those who envied her and repeated scandal about her out of envy; and in the Toronto nights Sidonia would talk about Sabina, the police informer from the time after the Czech uprising in 1848, who even after a century and a half was held up as the archetypal stool pigeon and a symbol of moral filth, even though he also wrote the libretto for *The Bartered Bride*, the nation's most popular musical.

"Forgotten," Sidonia would say, "but if it comes in handy ..." As indeed it did, later, to the shame of the nation to which we had once belonged. Not in Sidonia's case, because after her court victory she did not demand any libel money from her detractors, but in the fates of other people condemned by gossips with no proof except that their names were on the List— gossips who first made sure they themselves weren't there, and when they did not find themselves among the ostracized, launched their righteous campaign of vilification. "It's not a matter of forgetting," Sidonia would say during those nights in our beautiful city on Lake Ontario. "I don't want people to forget. I want to be pure. And I shall never be pure, never again in my life." So she tortured herself, my wife.

All of this passed through my mind as I stood before the judge, and everything that had preceded it, as I'd once tried to summarize it in my secret speech in the tile-covered house of the Interior Ministry: everything that later became the stuff of the beautiful novel Sidonia would eventually write in America. But no one else present knew Sidonia's history, except Lester, who may also have been remembering times past as he waited in the courthouse corridor in his winter coat, his moustache standing out from the raised collar; a few memories, perhaps, flashed through Juliette's mind, but she knew very little about Sidonia's old life, in the terrifying residence with the nightmarish latrine, because she had been young then, unobservant, and moreover wore the ideological glasses her political instructor, Sochova, had put on her nose. I'm sure something of the kind also went through Sidonia's brother Mirek's head, as he stood in his winter coat next to Lester, waiting to be called as a witness.

We were witnesses, but nonwitnesses. My testimony, perhaps, was acceptable, since I had lived with Sidonia for almost forty years, and I had been the prime mover of the devilish mechanism of suspicion: so I told the judge the entire story, as it actually happened. But only the late Sedlacek could have corroborated Sidonia's statement that she had not signed any Faustian pact. I only talked, even though what I said was true; but truth is usually indistinguishable from the well-rehearsed lie. Those three—the female judge, the Ministry's representative, and even our lawyer—kept what they thought to themselves.

Mirek said much less than I. What could he have said? At the time of Sidonia's "crime" he was in a concentration camp, and he had been there for almost ten years before the crime, and almost three years afterwards. He was just a character witness; he testified that his little sister, from whom he had been parted when she was fifteen and whom he hadn't seen again until she was almost thirty, had always been a good girl: how she shared her apple with him, when Mom had scraped some pennies together to buy an apple. All he did was narrate that Dickensian novel from a different angle. However, in people's minds, forty years of Party-told stories about onetime social misery changed Mirek's narrative from fact into a dubious legend. The judge, the Ministry's representative and our lawyer, all born about the time of the Party coup in 1948, looked at Sidonia's brother, a former political prisoner, as if they were viewing a character from that legendary time.

Juliette? She too was a character witness and not much else. Sidonia had always been an excellent friend, etc. However, her testimony contained one fact: Juliette had indeed dated Markovic, the lad of the politically incorrect nationality. Nothing had happened to her because of that flirtation, although something might well have, for in that era things often happened to unsuspecting people. And in that bygone time, the trio who were now to decide the matter had been holding on to Mother's apron strings, or more likely memorizing prayers in the kindergarten to the saints of those peculiar times.

That was what went through my mind. The judge studied the yellowed paper with a frown on her face, and eventually she turned to the Ministry's representative.

"Do you have anything else, doctor?"

He didn't. Not even a negative character witness. Just that one yellowed page of paper, and the judge obviously was not of Doc. Dr. Adolf Hrabe, Dr. Sc's radical persuasion. After an extremely short deliberation she passed the verdict in the name of the state where Sidonia and I no longer lived. She declared that the report on the best friend did not provide a sufficient reason for dismissing Sidonia's charge against the Ministry of the Interior, and so Sidonia won. Together with Julie, Lester and Mirek we went to drink her health in a pub I vaguely remembered, mainly because of the headwaiter, who had been there in the old days and was there still, and who, like me in another country, had grown old.

I WAS HEADED FOR THE BOOZE SHOP, AS MY OLD countrymen called government liquor stores, in the mall of the Hudson's Bay Company, passing on the way another shop whose wares also brought comfort to people. "The Anti-Aging

Store"—my old countrywomen had no nickname for it yet—promised to stop the biological process that leads naturally to silver hair, breasts responding too much to the force of gravity, and tires round people's bellies. As a sideline, the establishment removed tattoos. I stopped at that last bastion of politically incorrect females and looked at a lonely container with some wonder-cream, a container sitting in an aesthetically attractive shop window, designed probably by a graduate of some art school. The cream guaranteed the removal of wrinkles within three days or your money back. Out of the corner of my eye I saw the brass doorhandle glitter and turn, and then my student of detective stories appeared, in the pretty uniform of Canadian female cops. She had visited the anti-aging shop probably because of her hardly visible extra pounds, or perhaps there was a tattoo somewhere on her body that had met the fate of Wayne Hloupee's belly beauty. She saw me and saluted, touching her elegant hat. I thought she looked slimmer.

"Well, well," I said. "Had a tattoo removed, Sergeant Sayers?"

"Who told you?" The sergeant frowned.

"My usual informer," I answered. "The carrot-top."

She seemed relieved and said, "No tattoo. I came here because of my problem. You remember what it is, don't you?"

In a courteous way I looked over her diminished proportions.

"Not much of a problem any more."

"Thank you," she said in the polite customary way of the country where we lived now. "They sell a new diet here, and it seems to be working. Don't you think?"

She wanted to hear again that she'd slimmed down.

"You bet it's working," I assured her. "But now, in spite of your diet, can I buy you a cup of coffee?"

In the little cafeteria she explained that the regime was based on a pill, expensive for sure, but effective, to be taken thrice daily. The allowed food consisted of one carrot and two celery sticks in the morning and again in the evening.

"Have you tried carrot and celery sticks without the pill?" I asked.

She shook her head. "The diet wouldn't work then."

"But have you tried?"

She answered, guiltily, "Yes."

"And?"

"I became terribly hungry. I couldn't control myself and had to have a snack."

"The pill makes you lose your appetite?"

"It doesn't. But I manage not to eat."

"Just as a matter of interest," I said, "how much do you spend on the diet?"

"Quite a lot. About thirty bucks weekly. But it works."

It was a considerably overpriced placebo. I changed the subject: "Have you finished your story?"

"Almost." She became silent. She probably hadn't written anything.

"Will it still have that remote control device?"

She looked at me with a reproach in her eyes. "Don't you remember, sir? You allowed me to leave Uncle Abner and return to Poe?"

"I did?"

"Yes. You said the Locked Room Mystery had only nine solutions, and they'd become boring for you."

"Did I say that?"

"You suspect me of lying?" she said in her official voice. "You *did* say it!"

I did not wish her to suspect me of thinking ugly things about her, so I hastened to ask, "Well, what about the Poe-esque scenario? The one you had almost finished?"

For a moment, the sergeant didn't answer. Then she said, "I'm waiting for confirmation of the key fact." Again she fell silent, looking at the remains of the coffee at the bottom of her cup. Then she raised her eyes to meet mine. "You were right, sir. There was a hired gun."

It amazed me that I'd hit the bullseye. At the moment, I couldn't remember what had prompted me to form the hypothesis.

"Did you catch him?"

She shook her head. "We only know who it may have been. We're waiting for San Francisco to check whether he has an alibi for that night."

"C'mon," I said. "You can tell *me*. Who is it?"

Suddenly I remembered who inspired me to come up with the hypothesis. But he wouldn't do it for money.

"His name is Cotton Mather," said the sergeant. "He is Professor Mather's younger brother."

THEY IDENTIFIED HIM USING STATE-OF-THE-ART techniques: he popped up on the FBI computer. He bore the name of a famous witch-hunting ancestor, but was the black sheep of the family. Strictly speaking, he wasn't even a hired killer. As an eighteen-year-old, he dreamed about a Cadillac convertible, but lacked funds. His father refused to help him, for that year he had bought a new car for the family and given one to each of his two sisters. Luckily, a rich schoolfellow with a problem appeared: a Mike MacBeth. He was Cotton's friend and the star of the school's football team. Over two beers in the pub across the street from the school, where everybody went to meet with the local drug dealer, MacBeth told Cotton a secret: their beautiful colleague from high school, Veronica Marten, whom they both admired, had been made pregnant by the football star. And MacBeth made the simple and well-known discovery: as soon as the old-fashioned Veronica gave him the order to marry her, he realized the truth of the saying that beauty is in the eye of the beholder. The pretty Veronica grew ugly, and MacBeth's love for her, or whatever it was, evaporated. He suggested abortion: not at the local abortion clinic, which was used mainly by poor black women, but in the fancy baby-killing establishment of a famous gynecologist in the state capital. MacBeth came from old money and could pay. However, the girl believed in the Christian God and wouldn't be convinced that the "stupid piece of living shit in her vagina," as her lover angrily called the future baby, was no more a human being than a tapeworm. And so in the pub that night the two agreed to a deal: the football star would be rid of the bride, and Cotton would get a car. Strictly speaking, the bride herself was not to disappear, only the necessity of marrying her. Cotton, properly disguised in a stocking mask (they both knew, from television, how the deed should be done) was to lie in wait for the girl and, at the proper moment, hit her on the belly with a baseball bat, so that the living piece of shit would leave her body.

Everything went like a TV show, except that the living shit did not leave the girl's body and the girl died of shock. An autopsy established that she had a large bruise on her belly and a weak heart. And also that she was pregnant. The local homicide detective unravelled the case in no time when the two admirers of the late schoolgirl, whose passion for her was a public secret, became hopelessly entangled in contradictory statements.

So Cotton wasn't actually a hired killer, but what he did was enough to earn him ten years in the cooler. Since the verdict, his oldest sister Mary hadn't shown her face in their native town. She kept the skeleton well locked in her closet. After serving half of his sentence the younger brother was released on parole, but the experience of jail made him a drifter, a junkie and generally a good-for-nothing freeloader. A witness saw him leaving Professor Mather's house about two days before the murder, but he hadn't been seen in town since.

"Well, I don't know," I said to the sergeant. "Basically, it confirms our hypothesis. But the identity of the hired gun ... I don't know."

Because I had a different killer in mind, and he wouldn't do it for money.

He had a very good salary and job offers from several universities.

THE TRIAL WAS OVER, SIDONIA HAD WON, AND WE went to celebrate in the nearby pub where I remembered the waiter. A few hours later, soused to the gills, we were driven in Lester's car, by Juliette, because she was almost sober, as far as the tenement house where her children were expecting her. After a brief discussion about who should be entrusted with our lives and limbs for the next stage of our trip, Mirek, a former Prague cabbie, took the wheel, and almost overturned the car on the bank of the Moldau River. I was sitting with Lester in the back, Sidonia next to her big brother in front, and Lester was telling me about his hypothesis of how he'd gotten onto the List.

Shortly before the Velvet Revolution, he had gone to make a regular business report to his boss, Servac, who was a comrade but "otherwise a decent fellow," as such people were characterized. During the meeting a man unknown to Lester was sitting in the boss's office. Servac introduced him as Comrade Prochazka. The generic name gave Lester no hint, and using the common prefabricated clichés Lester described some business meeting in the West, where he'd succeeded in closing a deal with a producer of CDs who specialized in baroque music. The producer was represented by a certain Arnulf Berholz from Munich, who was pleasant to deal with and had, to employ a buzzword current in Prague at that time, a positively open mind.

Suddenly, Comrade Prochazka spoke up. "You also closed a deal with him last year at Fedaso at Cannes. Am I right, comrade?"

He was right. Lester knew it, and it occurred to him that while introducing Prochazka Servac hadn't identified him in any specific way. Also that Prochazka was suspiciously well informed. To gain time for some quick thinking he said, as if he did not comprehend, "Fedaso?"

"Festival of Dantseh Songs," said Comrade Prochazka with Czech pronunciation. "And while you were there, you had a meeting with Plantner."

Lester tried hard to remember who from Prague besides himself was at Fedaso that time and might have ratted on him. He couldn't remember anyone.

"Really?" he asked like an idiot.

"It has been reported to us."

"I think that Plantner attended a party given by Steinmetz Verlag," Lester conceded.

"He did. And then you invited him to your hotel room."

Plantner was an employee of Radio Free Europe, and as such was a dangerous person for citizens of the state where Sidonia and I had once lived. Lester therefore denied the invitation to the hotel room. And at the same time he remembered that Berholz had come to visit him unannounced. Because Lester had not suspected Berholz of any connections in Prague other than business ones, he introduced him to Plantner. Then, as Lester wrote in the report, from which he naturally omitted Plantner, they had spent some time in convivial conversation. Before Berholz appeared unannounced in his room, Lester had submitted another report to the man from Radio Free Europe, but except for Berholz nobody in Cannes had seen Lester in Plantner's presence; the radio reporter was too experienced to approach Lester in public. He had phoned to ask for a meeting, and the StB hardly had enough money to bug the Cannes Grand Hotel. Then Lester realized that lately Berholz had been spending more time in Prague than in Munich, and that his Prague business was growing remarkably.

"And last year, as you were in the Youesah, comrade," continued the fink, "on that private trip by invitation, you met Plantner in California."

"I think he came to my lecture," Lester admitted feebly, but Comrade Prochazka seemed to have lost interest in the man from Radio Free Europe.

Two days later, Lester got a summons to present himself at the building where, eons earlier, I had tried to help Sidonia. It was still in full operation. The meeting was factual and interesting. Comrade Prochazka and another comrade alternately read from Lester's reports to Servac, and here and there compared them with some other reports. From the comparison it became obvious that Lester's reports were incomplete. Certain people—not, however, people "of a special coinage," as Party members liked to call themselves—were missing from the reports.

"Man," I sighed, and a wave of immense sadness enveloped me. "So you signed," I said in a very subdued voice, lest Sidonia hear.

"Man," said Lester, "I shat my pants full, but not above my waist."

"So you didn't sign?"

"No," said Lester. "But man," my old buddy told me, "in my stupidity I had no idea that Servac was forwarding my reports. He had always been a comrade, but otherwise a decent fellow."

And in the drunken jalopy driven by Sidonia's brother, the political ex-prisoner, I realized for the first time that Servac, although certainly an informer, was not on the List. That people of that special coinage, members of the Party, weren't there at all. Except those who had been expelled from the club, like the onetime silly *poeta laudator* Vrchcolab, who had supported the revisionist Dubcek.

But Servac, quite rightly, was not on the list of agents. He was no agent; he certainly never signed anything. He was just doing his Party duty.

Mirek, the onetime cabbie, drove through the closed gate of Lester's family house and stopped an inch before the steps.

Suddenly I was sober.

AT LESTER'S WE WATCHED THE VIDEO THAT CLEOPATRA had brought to the courthouse. In the establishing shot, the one that introduces the general theme of the movie, a little animal appeared; it was a beautiful specimen of the resourceful creature, known to every schoolchild, that can change its colour.

Ostensibly the movie respected the democratic maxim *audiatur et altera pars*, and let even those it presumed guilty speak for themselves. There were several wise men of Mr. Mrkvicka's type, who gravely discussed the moral depravity of people on the List. These included the ruddy-faced Mr. Mrkvicka himself and various of his sidekicks. In the old days a team like that would suffice, since no dissenting opinions were allowed. But since now we lived in a democracy, a few rather incoherent token suspects were given bits of screen time, and because there was no way to prove or disprove anything, they only denied their involvement. Mr. Mrkvicka & Co. also only asserted without proofs, but psychology plays strange tricks. Both unproved assertions and unproved denials leave the same aftertaste in your mind: "It was probably not exactly like that, but there must be something to it." That piece of shit at the bottom of the cesspool.

Anyway, the ancient principle of hearing both sides can easily be circumvented by film editing. Pinko U.S. television would show Reagan giving a speech, but the editing would not permit him to finish his sentence, so that the American president appeared confused, like the former boss of Czechoslovakia whose mental qualities Sidonia's mother, many years ago, had questioned. The method was related to the trick known in literature as quoting out of context.

Cleopatra's film demonstrated it with Sidonia. For her new opus, Cleopatra had borrowed a piece from the documentary about Sidonia's honorary doctorate shot in the summer of the previous year in Toronto. I remembered the event well: it was only a few days earlier, during the dinner with Suzi, that Sidonia had learned she was on the List. Consequently, for most of the shooting time she was in a state heavily marked by symptoms brought on by whisky. In the shot Cleopatra selected for her chameleon film these were clearly visible.

I knew my countrymen from the land where Sidonia and I had once lived. A famous woman under the influence, and on the screen at that, didn't make a good impression, although everybody loved guzzlers on the screen if they were acting in a comedy. Even viewers who were personally well acquainted with double vision were unfavourably affected by a publicly soused well-known woman.

As we watched Cleopatra's film, I looked at Sidonia from the corner of my eye. She firmly held her glass, filled with the liquid that causes those symptoms, and stared at her own picture on the screen. When the shot ended, Lester began to grumble, because he remembered the film about Sidonia's doctorate, and Mirek, who had inherited openness from his mother, said aloud, "The swine!" He, too, remembered the movie from which the shot was taken.

It was a good example of film editing. In the older movie Sidonia was explaining how Sedlacek had tried to talk her into writing a report on Juliette, who was suspected of class misalliance, and how it suddenly occurred to her that by doing so she could help her friend. In the new film, Cleopatra skillfully edited out the sentence, "And so it occurred to me suddenly that I could give Julie a hand." She left in the sentence, "And so I wrote it." And she omitted the closing sentence, "And I made Markovic into a Bulgarian." The result was strictly according to Eisenstein.

We forgot about sobering up that afternoon, and later that night Sidonia, Mirek and I took a taxi to our hotel. Not that Lester would have been afraid to lend us his car, but at that time he was beyond fear and trembling, lying on the floor under the piano.

SO FAR NEITHER CAPTAIN WEBBER NOR HIS ASSISTANT had been able to crack the Hammett case, because Cotton Mather's alibi proved to be rather complicated. Cotton explained his absence from San Francisco on the day of the murder and for three days afterwards by asserting that he had spent all that time with friends at their cottage in the deep forests of Vancouver Island. Unfortunately, both his hosts left the cottage one day after he'd departed, and he didn't know where they went. The FBI started a chase, so far with no result.

The case was at a dead end. Professor Mather didn't deny that her brother had come for a one-hour visit two days before the murder of her husband, but since both she and her spouse were allergic to him, she gave him a considerable sum of money, as he demanded, to get rid of him.

The sergeant and her boss were also unable to break the mutual alibi of Kelly and Brown, who'd spent the fatal night together at the Xanadu motel; a drunken guest confirmed it. He was banging on their door at nine-thirty at night and demanded entry. They were both in the room, undressed and in bed. Kelly put on a dressing gown and dragged the inebriated gentleman to his own chamber where an impatient wife was already waiting for him. She had briefly spoken to Kelly and vouched for his alibi.

That put an end to the Hercule Poirot hypothesis: that the two had conspired to murder Hammett, and that after they registered at the motel at nine, Kelly slipped out through the window, drove to the Mather residence, strangled Hammett, returned and climbed back in through the window at about ten o'clock. The coroner's report fixed the time of the murder as nine at the latest, or at about the time the two were registering at the motel.

The suspects had all been eliminated now, and Captain Webber couldn't think of anyone else. Except possibly Robert Browning, the shy student whom Cooper had failed in math—Sergeant Sayers thought that he might be the hired gun.

I was amazed. "Browning?"

I recalled the bespectacled student and how he had opened the door of Cooper's office, where Cooper had been doing something with Candace Quentin; and how he had quickly closed the door again and retreated, exclaiming in a near-whisper, "Sorry! I'll come later!"

"Browning," confirmed Sergeant Sayers with a logic akin to that of Mr. Mrkvicka. "Let's suppose he was mad at Cooper, and confided in Mather. Then she promised him an A if he murdered her husband."

"Don't you think it's rather improbable?"

"You told us, didn't you, that after we had eliminated everything that was impossible, whatever remained, however improbable, must be the truth."

"That was not me but Sherlock Holmes. And only allegedly—"

Nevertheless, the sergeant clung to her curious hypothesis and eventually made Captain Webber summon the scared Browning, but the moment Webber saw him, and heard his voice vibrating like a tortured violin string, he dismissed him and told the sergeant something very unkind and unjust. But what it was she refused to tell me.

WHEN I ENTERED THE FACULTY CLUB, MARY MATHER was sitting there alone. I asked her politely whether she was expecting anyone, and she said she was—a colleague from Cornell who was to act as an examiner at some doctoral defence. At that point I forced myself on her company. She looked disapprovingly at my Manhattan, and I offered her my belated condolences for the demise of her husband.

She thanked me and said, "To make matters worse, I am being harassed by the police. They suspect me of having had something to do with Raymond's murder."

"My God! Not really!" I faked abhorrence.

"Why else should I have to prove my alibi?"

"That's a mere formality. After a murder, everybody close to the victim has to provide an alibi. It doesn't mean anything."

"Well," Mather said, "you teach detective stories. Anyway, I feel insulted."

I assured her of my sympathy, but repeated that the checking of alibis after a murder was routine business. Then I sipped at my Manhattan and sighed sentimentally. "Your husband was still alive when we talked last."

"When was that?"

"On the plane to Chicago. We both flew to conferences there."

"Oh, yes," she appeared to have some difficulty recalling the episode. "That was a long time ago."

It was less than a semester, but I did not correct her.

"We talked about the paper you intended to read at your conference."

"I don't remember that."

"You told me that, basically, it would be an obituary of Professor Pasternak and that you would be quoting from a letter your cousin had sent you shortly before his death."

"From a letter?" she seemed astonished, but then remembered again. "But of course. You're right. I quoted some passages from that letter."

"You said that the paper was to culminate in a mathematical *pointe*."

"Did I? Now that you tell me—I did have an idea, but on further thought it came to nothing. My paper was a straight obituary. There was no *pointe*."

I knew that much from Oskar. But my memory was better than hers. She consulted her wristwatch and said, "I must go. I have an important meeting that I cannot possibly miss. Will you do me a favour?"

"Certainly."

"When my colleague from Cornell arrives, would you tell him that I waited for him for an hour and a half, but that I had to leave? He should kindly go to the desk at Hart House; his room has been reserved."

She got up.

"I hope I'll know him when I see him," I said.

"He comes always with his very pretty wife. I'm sure you'll notice *her*."

Was she really capable of irony? Was her stress on the wife a scoffing allusion to my interest in kittens?

"His name is Professor Oskar Plawetz," she said dryly, and left the club.

In less than five minutes, Oskar's very pretty wife appeared with her large purse but without Oskar. She noticed me immediately, for I was still alone in the club, and joyfully joined me. I gave her Mather's message.

"Oskar had a seizure," she said. "We already had been to our room at Hart House, but then Oskar had this seizure and couldn't keep the appointment with Mrs. Mather."

"I hope it's nothing serious?"

"Come on! Don't you know Oskar? He convinced himself that he was having a heart attack. I was unable to talk him out of it, so I had to call an ambulance. Naturally it was no heart attack. He ate both his and my lunch on the plane and got heartburn."

"Is he in bed?"

"No. He's in the men's room. He mixed his regular pills with some junk they gave him for the heartburn in the airport drugstore, and now he is sitting in the john. But he will join me, never fear."

As soon as the last word passed her lips, Oskar Plawetz entered the club.

THE JOURNAL *KILL KOMMUNISM!* DID WHAT I HAD expected. Sidonia's legal victory didn't count with them, and they supported their dismissal of it with a whole collection of arguments. Not even a rather classical *argumentum ad hominem* was missing from their repertoire, which I had also expected. The real character of Sidonia was best documented, wrote a new contributor named Jan Koec, by the film that was supposed to throw a favourable light on her. Instead, in at least one scene, she appeared visibly not sober. The correspondent Skrzkrk, whom I knew already, combined the conclusions of the blonde Ministry lawyer with the old contention of the now silent Doc. Dr. Adolf Hrabe, Dr. Sc., and asserted first that judges did not understand the specifics of the List, and second that Sidonia had, however unwittingly, become an StB agent the moment she wrote the report on Julie Tyburc, no matter how favourable it was. Koec's and Skrzkrk's judgements were further elaborated by a reader who signed his name as P.S.: according to him, today's judges understood the specifics of the List only too well, but they were all Communists, and were finding for the plaintiffs, and thus crossing their names off the List, thereby defending their own people against the present Ministry of the Interior. P.S.'s contention, I gathered, was that there were no Communists employed by the present Ministry—which would contradict the prevailing theories of the journal. According to those, even Sidonia's old friend, now the president, was a Communist and an StB agent. The *faux pas* had probably escaped the editor. Another contributor, Dr. Otto Skorzeny, was of the opinion that, according to some leaks printed in various papers over the past five years, the StB had destroyed a substantial part of their files, since they felt endangered. As proof he mentioned the black smoke allegedly rising from the chimneys of the StB building in the Moravian capitol of Brno and invoked the metaphor of there being no smoke without fire. He opined that the incompleteness of the fire-damaged archival material explained why nothing else had been found in Sidonia's file except the report she had talked about in several interviews. However, that in no way proved, wrote Dr. Skorzeny, that *originally* (Dr. Skorzeny's italics) there had not been other documents in the file, much less innocent. For instance, a signed agreement to work as agent. But since it was generally known that StB agents were protecting their own people even today, some of them very likely had removed the harmful document from Sidonia's papers and left only the report on Tyburc to support the credibility of Sidonia's defence.

The hypothesis was of the "Put Your Cards on the Table, Mrs. Sidonia!" variety. But from the point of view of strict logic, no objections could be raised against the possibility of Sidonia's file being incomplete. Only I knew that it was complete, but I felt no inclination to mail an affidavit to *Kill Kommunism!* If for no other reason than because Doc. Dr. Adolf Hrabe, Dr. Sc. might emerge from his temporary silence and sneeringly remind me that such an affidavit had no legal validity, since the defendant (Dr. Hrabe and some other correspondents, in a Freudian slip, often changed Sidonia's status from plaintiff to defendant) was my wife. To enter into discussion with the authors of *Kill Kommunism!* would be like entering a vicious circle. In the state where Sidonia and I had once lived, nothing was provable and there were no juries. Even if Jesus Christ Himself appeared above Prague, as the hero's *yiddishe momma* arose over Manhattan in a film by Woody Allen, and declared that Sidonia was innocent of all charges, the surrealists of *Kill Kommunism!* would argue that another of Sidonia's old friends, now a famous American movie director, had supplied her with Hollywood special-effects magicians to conjure up the appearance.

The journal closed its anthology with another bit of borrowing from the Ministry's blonde. Mr. Mrkvicka could not comprehend what Sidonia "and her ilk" wanted to achieve. An entry in the register of files, or if you preferred, in the List, did not prove that the person entered had behaved like an agent. It proved solely that he or she had been entered in the files.

Mr. Mrkvicka didn't elaborate on the *verbatim* quote. What a name on the List proved in the country where I and Sidonia had once lived, his paper was proving week after week.

But Sidonia wasn't particularly troubled by this carnival of absurdities. What hit her like an exploding grenade had happened before her court victory, and Mr. Mrkvicka's journal was not directly responsible for it.

"HI!" SAID OSKAR PLAWETZ, AND FELL EXHAUSTED INTO the chair next to his wife. Turning to her, he whispered, "Marcella, give me the Kaopectate!"

"Charcoal helped you last time," said Marcella, and handed him a vial full of black pills.

Oskar studied the fine print on the label. "This cannot be taken with other drugs. It neutralizes their effect. Give me the Kaopectate!"

The plastic bottle with the intestinal cement also had directions for use, and Marcella studied them. "It's exactly the same," she said. "It weakens the effect of other medication."

"What shall I do?" whimpered her husband.

"You should stuff yourself with chocolate," I advised him. "It will cement your intestines just like Kaopectate, but it won't block the effect of your other drugs, except penicillin."

"I don't take penicillin. I'm allergic to it." Oskar looked around. "Do you think they sell chocolate here?"

"They sell Bols chocolate liqueur."

I spent the next hour in convivial conversation with Marcella. She knew everyone in the theatre business in Prague, and amazingly—or maybe not that amazingly—in the literature business as well. She was even acquainted with Sidonia's friend the president; so we never ran out of subjects. There was also something I wanted to ask Oskar about, but he was too busy cementing his intestines with Bols liqueur. It brought on amnesia and he forgot to take his pills, although the purse kept ringing, and alcohol would not block their effectiveness.

As we said our goodbyes in the hall (the club was in Hart House), I asked Oskar, "Listen, who found Mortimer Pasternak when he died? The newspapers said that he'd been discovered in his office by a colleague. Was it you?"

Oskar swayed but Marcella held him firm.

"Not me—I wasn't—" he blabbered. "It was that guy from your college—you know the guy, they called that theorem after him ... damn, I can't remember ..."

CHAPTER TEN

The Opinion Poll of the

Prague Literary Weekly,

and the Case Begins

to Clear Up,

At Least for Me

THE INFORMATION WAS DUBIOUS, published clandestinely, in spite of the government's "top secret" label. But that didn't deter the *Prague Literary Weekly*. They printed an opinion poll about the guilt or innocence of the writers named in the List. I was stunned by how many engineers of human souls, except for a tiny minority, responded to the poll and how vehemently they condemned their colleagues who were alleged to have ratted to the StB. One would expect writers to be more thoughtful in their handling, if not of ideas, at least of words and their meanings, especially in a definite historical context. Nobody, except maybe finks, liked the StB informers. But on the authority of stories printed in an obscure tabloid, the engineers uncompromisingly denounced not colleagues who had been finks, but colleagues who appeared on the List, which, to quote the highest authority—the blonde lawyer—meant only that these individuals had been put on the List and nothing else. I had never studied semantics, but I was a writer—admittedly of mere detective stories, but still a writer. The semantic shift from the neutrally expressed hypocrisy of the Ministry lawyer to the angry public condemnation in the poll of the writers' weekly was painfully obvious.

Reading the swift judgements of colleagues who had once been *my* colleagues, I remembered Graham Greene, my famous friend and mentor; and his advice that a writer, because he is a writer, should focus not on characters whom everybody liked, but on heroes for whom there were no fingers crossed. And I remembered Ilona Kopanec, the mother of children of another husband, whose ratting activity had received such high marks from Vojtech Kysely, the former StB colonel who was now a successful private entrepreneur in Canada. But of course, the engineers didn't know Ilona's case; it was just my private information gained from a former secret agent who perhaps had developed pricks of conscience. Most of the engineers who had participated in the poll had no doubts. Reading the outpourings of their indignation over crimes for which they had no proofs, I just wasn't sure whether theirs was a failure of moral consciousness or of imagination, the trademark of their craft. That ability, as the old romantics believed, to put one's feet in other persons' shoes, which enabled ugly old men like Count Tolstoy to enter an unhappy woman's soul. But perhaps for that aptitude the engineers did not possess a diploma.

It was a horrifying failure. But it was what her own authors wrote that exploded like a fragmentation grenade in Sidonia's soul. Until very recently, with literal sweat on her brows, she had helped to bring to the world their Dickensian children

147

(as the great British master used to call his books) when in the country where she and I had once lived the Party government ruled supreme. All those children found refuge in her orphanage. She was like the good stepmother she had alluded to in her speech—and copies of that speech were desired by professors in the country where we now lived. Although Sidonia wasn't the real mother, she rejoiced in her children's success with the customers of her publishing venture, who were scattered over the wide, wide world by the blow of the armoured fist. She even worried when some of them found no understanding with her female readers. Although she was a mere stepmother, these children were her life.

THE FATHER OF TWO SUCH CHILDREN, LUKAS VARHOLA, had the reputation of a thinker, almost a sage. He suggested that something like a court of peers be established which would weigh the sins of the colleagues on the List and distribute punishments. Perhaps the suggestion was owing to his mental training of many years earlier, before he turned writer, for he, too, had been a man for whom the club reigning in the country coined the self-congratulatory term *of special coinage*.

And in those almost prehistoric times, in August 1968, shortly before the coming of the tanks, my old friend Ocenas and I were standing on a terrace above Prague, looking at the engineers assembled at a party given by Alexander Dubcek, who was then leader of the country. Ocenas and I debated why we too were not people of that coinage. Ocenas ventured that they had been young and stupid, and I countered by asking whether we had been old and wise? Later, at home, it dawned on me that we too had been young and stupid, but our stupidity damaged solely our own lives, not the lives of so many of our fellow men.

SIDONIA NEVER SPOKE ABOUT THOSE THINGS, although the club—for they were a private club, these unlimited rulers of our old country—had sent her brother for twelve years to the uranium mines, and chased her daddy away to America, where he was buried in some pauper's grave. When Sidonia was in New York she had tried to find the grave, but there was no trace of it.

The club also damaged the life of her two sisters: they entered the adult world without the benefit of higher education; they became workers, which—curiously in that country ruled over by people of special coinage—was a punishment. Sidonia herself escaped her sisters' fate because she married me (on orders from the StB, according to Mr. Mrkvicka) and, as my wife, penetrated the high society of the engineers. One of them, a friend, a professor at the Film Academy, had led her safely through various wrong-class-origin traps to admission to the school, from which she was later expelled by the armoured fist. The friend also left the country, soon after Sidonia and me, and achieved success and celebrity as a novelist. But above all, he became her author, and she became the stepmother of all his children, as long as they spoke their mother tongue. The famous friend knew his Graham Greene, and he never disappointed Sidonia. He stopped being an engineer of human souls many years ago.

LEONIE, SIDONIA'S FAVOURITE AUTHOR, WAS THE daughter of a man who for most of his life also was pleased to accept the designation *of special coinage*, so she was in no danger of class punishments like the ones dealt to Sidonia's sisters. Among men of his own stature, Leonie's father reached the highest echelons; he even regularly played poker at the Hradchin castle with Novotny, the president, so that a folk saying was born about the "momentary Karel Capek" whose qualities depended on the qualities of the "momentary Masaryk." However, Leonie's father never published his *Conversations with Novotny*, as Capek did his with Masaryk. He just played cards with the president. But then, Novotny's conversations consisted purely of Party jargon and would never have been a bestseller like Capek's book.

Then Leonie's father, too, was smashed by the armoured fist; but Leonie had already finished her education when she was demoted, as punishment, to the working class. She took the job of cleaning lady, and worked nights in a cinema.

Sidonia never spoke about Leonie's family, whose life and fate were so different from her own. When she published two of Leonie's books, she gave them even more than her usual care, perhaps out of female solidarity, which exists just as female malice does, but is stronger; or perhaps because Sidonia's women customers, out of female malice, used to find fault with Leonie's literary artefacts.

And after Mr. Mrkvicka's List, Leonie, undoubtedly with the best of intentions, wrote Sidonia a well-meaning letter, and the letter exploded in Sidonia's soul like shrapnel. You committed a sin, dear Sidonia, Leonie wrote, but we shall forgive you. She meant well. After her father had fallen from grace at the castle, Leonie for twenty years swept the floors of her cinema theatre, and Sidonia avoided that fate by leaving the country with me in time. And so Leonie forgave her—but for what? Wasn't her entire sin a stupid attempt to help a friend in danger? And did Leonie's *we* include people who had once contributed to the cruel treatment meted out to Sidonia's brother, her father and her entire family? The offer of forgiveness was soured by the two questions; it revealed an automatic credulity in Leonie, which should not exist in a writer, for all good writers know that the first idea that occurs must be rejected. Such unexamined impulses must be destroyed by the power of thought, and by heeding Graham Greene's maxim: that the writer must try to find out what sort of soul is in a person whom everybody shuns.

Ideas she had never given much thought to, feelings that never belonged to her repertoire of emotions, now rebelled in Sidonia: memories of her Dickensian childhood, known to the sage Varhola and Leonie only from literature, of being hungry and cold, of the horrifying latrine that gave both me and Sidonia nightmares, and still caused her automatic revulsion whenever she had to use a public washroom. What gave the sage and the daughter of the castle gambler the right to forgive her? Shouldn't *she* forgive *them*? They had participated in ugly deeds or, because of those deeds, lived on the sunny side of society, while Sidonia existed in that society on charity bestowed upon beggars.

To both of them, the sage and Leonie, Sidonia sent letters they probably did not hang in gilded frames. Eventually, however, she forgave them, since she had always been—as her brother, the former political prisoner, had told the judge—a good girl.

I SPOTTED CANDACE IN THE CROWD OF GIRLS mobbing the famous director in the foyer of the movie theatre. I stepped up to her: "I'll introduce you, shall I?"

"Oh, no!" Candace breathed, and turned pink. He was a very famous director. And when a woman says no she sometimes means yes; although if she does it is, of course, an exception from the law of nature.

The world-famous director was another of my old buddies. Once we had written a screenplay together, which was then killed by representatives of the Party government. Besides our old friendship, I appreciated very much that he'd used a quotation from one of my detective stories as an epigraph to his first filmed script; measured by the strict moral standards of the times, it was almost immoral. That work became a fully deserved international hit, one of the few from the country in which we used to live. Luckily, it was released at a time when the political ice began to break up, and his subsequent career, judged by our expectations then, was truly dazzling. He was courted by Hollywood and later decorated with two Oscars. In the years that elapsed after the movie made special for me by the quotation, he seduced a superhuman number of women, but was protected against the danger of serial Hollywood marriages by the wife he had left in Prague. She never divorced him, since she was a clever Czech girl.

Now he was attending the Toronto premiere of his new film, and although he appeared everywhere with his new black girlfriend, I knew that if I introduced our college beauty to him, he wouldn't be annoyed. He wasn't; he gave her the hypnotic smile of cinematographical success and added her to his entourage, from which I excused myself. That night, though, I was sure nothing would happen; the dark beauty certainly wouldn't let him out of her sight.

Nevertheless, when the Edenvale beauty entered the Lame Duck the next afternoon, I could see from her expression that her heart had been pierced by the symbolic arrow. From my throne at the bar I wiggled my finger at her, and she ran up to me with a smile. This time it did not have the usual hypnotic effect on me, because, for a change, it was genuine.

"How did you like the director?" I asked, and didn't even have to nod in the direction of the bartender; the presence of the Edenvale good-looks champion on his bar stool worked like an order.

"I liked him very much, sir! How come you know him?"

"We grew up together in the same reform school."

"Really?" she sighed, but immediately controlled herself. The Hollywood hypnosis stepped aside to make room for sophistication. "Is that a Czech joke?" she hissed through lips bent into the scornful curve I knew so well. "And according to you, 'Lili Marlene' was a Nazi song. I don't buy that."

I didn't launch into a discussion to dispel her illusion concerning the ethnic background of the woman who used to stand *bei der Laterne, bei dem grossen Tor*, but went straight to the heart of the matter. "I'll probably tell on you."

"Can you be more specific?" The curve became even more pronounced.

"I don't mean your unexpected excellence in math. You needn't worry about that."

"I'm not worrying. You know nothing about me." She sipped her whisky with great self-assurance. "Your friend, the director, never left the side of his African-American friend. They share a hotel room."

"I am constantly receiving lessons about contemporary *mores*, but I swear to you, that idea never entered my head."

"If I wanted to fuck your friend, I wouldn't do it in Toronto. He told me he had a farm in Connecticut."

O tempora!

"I do not recommend a visit to that farm."

"I don't need your recommendation."

But she did not get up to join her buddies with the riveted ears, who were all sitting at another table around Dewey, this time with no ring in her lower lip, but one in each nostril. Candace waved to the bartender, and so did I. For a long while we remained silent, and the beauty twisted a loose curl around her index finger. Eventually, after an eternity had passed, she asked, "Well, what is it you'll tell on me?"

"That Freddie Hamilton did not attend that party."

"What party?"

"The evening they murdered Raymond Hammett."

"Am I supposed to have been at a party?"

"You told me that you were. You said you thought Freddie Hamilton was there, too."

"I've no idea what you're talking about. I don't remember any such party." She stopped, thought a little, then amended her statement. "That doesn't mean, of course, that I was not at *some* party that night. I'm not socially inactive, sir."

"But you do remember how I gave you a ride to your dormitory."

"That ... well, yes."

Her selective recall had a certain logic to it. Given her social activity, it was natural that some party or other could have slipped her mind. But it didn't happen every day that a professor would drive her at midnight down the road from Cresthill to campus.

Then she made a mistake. "But I told you I wasn't sure whether Freddie Hamilton had attended that party."

"So you remember the party? You attended it?"

"Well ... yes."

"You didn't, Miss Quentin."

THAT EVENING SIDONIA FELL ASLEEP SOON AFTER SIX p.m., after emptying a gin bottle. I spent what remained of the evening watching once again Cleopatra's opus, which we'd brought home from Prague to Toronto. Again I saw the Interior Ministry blonde who, although a cunning lawyer, could not comprehend. Again I studied Cleopatra's editing technique, her subtle betrayal, which like the cuts of her Soviet masters falsified the truth without appearing to do so. I listened to statements of people from the List, alternated in unequal time segments with Mr. Mrkvicka's hypotheses presented as facts, and with more hypotheses of another worker from the Interior Ministry. This man demonstrated the complex and foolproof system of entries into the register, which excluded any possibility of falsification, and skillfully led the viewer to conclude that, in the state where Sidonia and I had once lived and where all government institutions were busy faking data, only the group to which he himself now belonged had always resembled St. John of the Truth.

A widow followed the bald-headed man from the Ministry. Her husband, whose name was not on the List, had been shot and killed while trying to escape from a concentration camp. To create an impression of objectivity she was superseded by the mother of another political prisoner, who *was* on the List and had also been shot and killed during an escape attempt. From time to time, the little, long-tongued animal with the independently moveable eyes appeared in the montage, each time in a different colour. It must have been apparent, even to people not as well trained in the interpretation of symbols as college professors, that the little creature was conveying a message, and that message obviously was: someone is lying. Certainly not the widow of the killed man who was not on the List, because she had his death certificate. The mother of the other killed man also had his death certificate, but that document did not say anything about how her son had gotten onto the List. So objectivity imperceptibly changed into something else, and even people acquitted by the courts imperceptibly began to resemble the cross-eyed animal.

Then Mr. Mrkvicka named a gentleman, not me, who had come to the editorial offices of *Kill Kommunism!* in a rage and threatened to sue, but had shut up quickly when the Interior Ministry lawyer confronted him with the contents of his file. The gentleman swore that the StB document was a falsification; but the viewer was subtly reminded that the Institution resembled St. John of the Truth. After the destruction of the furious gentleman the animal appeared again, this time all chequered.

On the screen, Mr. Mrkvicka didn't mention my visit to the offices of *Kill Kommunism!* Nor did he mention my threat of a legal suit. However, our lawyer sent a summons to the publisher of *Kill Kommunism!* and also to Mrs. Parsons in Toronto.

ANOTHER MINISTRY WORKER APPEARED ON THE SCREEN to demonstrate the negative of the previously shown positive.

He did not assert that an error in the register was a sheer impossibility. But even with all my training in the composition of detective stories, I was able to follow his logic for only half a take before becoming lost in his syllogisms. His final pessimistic deduction, however, seemed to be that it would never be possible to arrive at an *absolute* certainty, because of errors, the disappearance or death of agents, and the extensive damage to the files. Neither before nor after him did anybody appear in the film who applied the same standards of absolute uncertainty to the people on the List who were actually discussed, and nobody mentioned the effect of hearsay—not the blonde lawyer, the mother of the killed political prisoner, or the law professor, whose advice was most interesting: if a citizen thinks that the accusations against him are false, the result of a mistake or an unjustified conclusion, it is up to him to prove that the verdict should have been negative.

Cleopatra did not interview any expert on Soviet law to explain to the public the legal theories of Stalin's chief prosecutor Vishinsky, based on the same concepts as the pronouncements of the law professor. She just intercut her montage with the many-coloured animal. My sympathy for her, which had existed because of her jazzman of a husband, vanished entirely.

I SWITCHED OFF THE TV AND WENT TO THE BEDROOM. Sidonia was fast asleep on gin. I lay down and, in my mind, switched to another, older film. It showed Sidonia and me soaked through on a ridge in the Krkonose Mountains, on our walk to the warm and absolute coziness of Peter's chalet. In another take we danced at a ball in the Julda Fulda ballroom, Sidonia in an evening gown, embellished with glittering stuff unavailable in Prague in those days. I had spent two precious days in Paris, not in the Louvre or at the Deux Magots but in department stores, searching for the stuff because I loved Sidonia. Another take: our weekend cottage at Chlomek, Sidonia stuffing her head with the history of the cinema after her friend from the Film Academy, later a world-famous novelist, had led her through the minefield of class obstacles to admission. On that day in late summer 1968, with barely a month before the blow of the iron fist, I read with apprehension the writer-sage's public challenge to people to rise and remove the discredited members of the club from their cozy posts. As if he didn't understand the country that only yesterday had represented for him the utopian future. For me it had never meant that, because I understood it well, perhaps better than the sage; and fear gripped me by the neck. I was afraid that the club, which had almost crushed Sidonia when its members were young and stupid, would complete the job now, when its members had grown old but remained stupid.

I couldn't fall asleep. I got up quietly and went to Sidonia's studio. I switched on the screen of her word processor, and in the dim light I saw the text of her unfinished novel. I felt like crying. And I did. Perhaps because I was old, and the carefree rainy trip to the warmth and absolute coziness of Peter's chalet would never happen again.

"YOU WENT TO VISIT PROFESSOR MATHER THAT EVENING, perhaps to find solace there or because of a promised tutorial. Because Cooper had thrown you out after you had made him your offer."

"What offer?" Candace glowered at me.

"A very ancient one. In romantic novels, when a man declines that offer the woman leaves in tears."

She shifted her gaze from my face into her glass.

"Your tears were tears of rage and helplessness, not of unrequited love. The grades that Cooper threatened you with would be a serious obstacle to admission to law school."

In the corner of the pub, somebody started to plunk a guitar. Or rather to beat the instrument in a monotonous rhythm. I looked over my shoulder. It was one of the punctured youths, defamiliarized by an incredible number of rings pushed through the rim of his ears. Dewey Drake launched into a song, or rather a squeal, which kept the guitar's beat but was incomprehensible. I turned back to Quentin.

"And lo and behold!" I said with stage pathos. "Against all expectations, you wrote the final exam for an A-plus, and in the faculty club, Cooper praised your progress in mathematics."

"I *learned* the damned thing!"

"Yes, you did. Even to the point where your final mark for the course was also an A-plus, although if one respects the mandatory percentages, such a result is a mathematical impossibility. As you certainly know, since you made such progress in mathematics."

She didn't respond.

"Unless Cooper rewrote the Fs for all your term papers and made them into As."

No response. Only Drake's squeal.

"Your improbable progress is somehow linked with something you did in Professor Mather's house on the night I gave you the ride. Or perhaps something you saw there."

"The last time I set foot in that house was a year ago," replied Candace at long last. "Professor Mather was giving me private tutorials then."

"No. The last time you went there was the night somebody bumped off her husband."

She resorted to irony. "Would you kindly explain to me where this theory is supposed to lead?"

"Hypothesis, Miss Quentin. Theory rests on established facts. Hypothesis is merely guesswork. Educated guesswork, perhaps, but guesswork nevertheless."

No response. Dewey was joined by two ring-bearers with strong but not musical voices.

"A hypothesis can, of course, change into a theory, if some facts are established. For instance, we would have to establish who searched through Professor Mather's file cabinet, and left there a piece of peeled-off nail polish, the same colour as a chip of nail polish my wife found in my car when she was cleaning it. The car in which I had given you a lift."

"You're right, sir. It's merely a hypothesis."

"But it can grow into a theory. In Hammett's fist, the police found a button in the shape of a soccer ball, such as is commonly used on tweed jackets in England. Professor Cooper has the same buttons on his jacket. At a recent party, one of his buttons was hanging by a thread, for it had been badly sewed on. My wife Sidonia noticed that."

The squeal and roar in the corner of the pub began bothering me. I continued, "In Professor Mather's file cabinet, where police found the peeled-off nail polish, the proprietor of that polish left one of the files open. The name on the file was Mortimer Pasternak."

Quentin said in a bored voice, "I can't bear Dewey's squealing. Let's go out."

THE DAY BEFORE, SIDONIA HAD HAD A HANGOVER SO dreadful that it shocked me. She cured it in a homeopathic way, only instead of small quantities of the poison she used another bottle of gin. In the morning we found a fax from our Prague lawyer informing us that the witness Parsons from Canada hadn't shown up at the trial. According to the strange custom of the country where I and Sidonia had once lived, if witnesses didn't obey the summons, the judge adjourned the case indefinitely. In the lawyer's opinion, this meant at least six months, probably more, and if the witness once again failed to show up, the case would be adjourned perhaps to the end of the century. Parsons was seventy-five; by the end of our millennium she would be eighty-one, and she wouldn't show up again for reasons of advanced age, or death.

As I was leaving for school, Sidonia had worked her way through half of a new bottle.

THE SERGEANT CAME TO HER MORNING TUTORIAL AND glowed with happiness: my first thought was that the murderer had been apprehended and my hypothesis would burst like a bubble. Her happiness, however, did not originate in professional success, but in the strange change that had happened to her service uniform. Even I noticed that it was now too big for her.

"Carrot and celery sticks, in combination with the pill?" I asked, and I managed to sound gleeful, although there was no glee in me.

"Exactly!" she bloomed. "Twenty pounds! Just like Oprah!"

"How much did it cost you?"

"Four hundred and twenty-seven dollars and seventy-seven cents!"

I took a pocket calculator from my desk drawer (I kept it there for calculating percentages), and clicked in her information. She was following my action with deep interest.

"Twenty-one dollars and thirty-eight cents per pound. That's substantially more than sirloin steak."

She laughed as I'd never heard her laugh before, and said, with great good cheer, "I saved that sum on food."

"Turn around so that I can see you!" I squinted at the door, but it stood ajar as ordered. The sergeant commenced her revolution; the uniform was hanging limply on her, even at the back, where a hefty female behind used to fill it. She kept turning around for me to get my fill of her newly achieved slimness. It probably beat Oprah.

Professor Ann Kate Boleyn, the sex officer, passed my door, stopped and with a scowl observed the pirouetting girl.

"Do you notice, Professor Boleyn, how much weight the sergeant has lost?" I said promptly. Sayers stopped turning round and gave Boleyn a toothy smile.

"I don't," said Boleyn with malice. "Besides, according to the timetable on your door you should now be giving her a tutorial."

She about-faced and marched away, her head held high.

"But you notice it, don't you, sir?" asked the sergeant unhappily.

"The uniform fits you as it would fit a scarecrow. Being a woman, Professor Boleyn should have noticed it."

"Did you?"

"As soon as you entered my office. Between you and me," I said, lowering my voice, "by leaving the door open we disappointed Professor Boleyn. She couldn't go into action."

"Should I close the door?"

"Better not. You'll see, she'll be back. If the door was shut, she would report me. And take a seat."

The sergeant sat down next to my desk, and we waited in silence. I was right in my estimation of the ideological worker. In a little while, and in the opposite direction, Boleyn passed my door again.

"O.K. Show me what you've written," I said as Boleyn was throwing a sharp glance through my open door.

"Nothing," she answered honestly. "You see, sir, the case does not evolve according to your hypothesis. What if I switch from reality to something like the Locked Room again?"

"The case doesn't evolve according to my hypothesis?"

"It doesn't. You see, that hired killer—they found the two guys who had been with Cotton Mather in the cottage on Vancouver island. Now he has an alibi."

"Oh, I see," I said.

"May I go back to the Mystery of the Locked Room, sir?"

"If you wish. But I wouldn't give up so easily. All Mather's alibi probably means is that the hired gun was someone else."

"But who?"

"Investigate, think, deduce. I won't tell you more."

The sergeant left, undecided whether she should hold on to Poe or to Uncle Abner. For her next tutorial, however, she brought me a new version of the mystery based on the remote-control device, reworked in the direction of such improbability that even after the elimination of all that was impossible, what remained still could not have been the truth.

WHEN I CAME HOME AT NOON, SIDONIA WAS ASLEEP again, and on the coffee table stood the empty bottle. I didn't wake her, and an hour later I drove back to Edenvale, where I stayed until evening. When I returned home Sidonia was awake, sitting at the kitchen table with a new bottle, three-quarters empty. I attempted a sermon, naturally with no result.

At night I thought about how on summer evenings we used to sit on the terrace outside her beautiful office; the setting sun shining on the clean North American sky, Sidonia reading proofs, and me smoking a big cigar. In those rare moments on the terrace we felt good because of our common work.

Then Communism went bust in Prague. The publishing firm became redundant, and suddenly Sidonia had nothing to do. Then she received the Order of the White Lion. Then the List came.

I did not sleep, just lay in my bed. Beside me Sidonia was breathing heavily, and a prick of conscience brought to my mind again my stupid attempt to help, which more than thirty years later led to the revelation.

I shook my head, and in my mind I saw Sidonia in her worn corduroy overcoat, walking from a trolley car towards me at the city corner of Wenceslas Square, to meet me for our first date. Smiling at me with her large brown eyes.

I covered my head with the blanket so that she would not hear me cry.

CHAPTER ELEVEN

The Two Murders

WALKED WITH CANDACE QUENTIN along a path called Eight Minutes Walk, because students were supposed to get from the smaller college building to the main one in approximately that time. We were in no hurry. I explained my hypothesis to her; by now it had been partly transformed into theory. From time to time I squinted at the girl's youthful face. At irregular intervals, illuminated by sunlight filtering through green maple leaves, the face was made even more beautiful by a cinematic effect; I remembered Sidonia's then equally youthful face in the light of neon signs and street-lamps on the city corner of Wenceslas Square. Long ago, long ago.

"On the fatal night," I said, "Professor Cooper was in Mary Mather's house. When he departed, he left behind Hammett's corpse and, in Hammett's stiff fist, a button. You were there, too. You left a bit of peeled-off nail polish in Professor Mather's file cabinet, open at *Mortimer Pasternak*."

"It's still only a hypothesis," said Candace.

"But it rests on two points I have just mentioned: the button and the nail polish. You won't find such beautifully tangible clues in many detective stories. The hypothesis is now half theory."

Professor Ann Kate Boleyn walked past, but since Quentin and I were in plain sight, she again couldn't spring into action.

"You arrived at the house, probably to ask Professor Mather for emergency tutorials, or perhaps to appeal to her to put in a word for you with Professor Cooper. You know why, I don't. It was almost dark, and when you entered the driveway, you saw Cooper's car. It's a brand-new Mercedes-Benz. He paid for the expensive vehicle with money earned by lecturing. Invitations rained on him, and his rate was never less than three thousand bucks."

Freddie Hamilton appeared on the path with a thick book under his arm. When he saw us, he disappeared into the foliage and spied on us from that vantage point as we continued to walk.

"Cooper surged to prominence because of the paper he had read at the Chicago conference. It contained the formulation of his theorem. And from that stemmed all the opulent honoraria. Cooper had become an academic star."

Candace walked silently at my side. She wore a flowered blouse and a plain blue skirt. She knew that her natural beauty didn't need to be embellished by an ox ring in the nose or tattoos in intimate places. On our first date, long ago, Sidonia had come in her worn corduroy overcoat with a grey beret on her head; the air on the Petrin hill was freezing, so that little ice crystals were bursting everywhere. When I took her to the Loretta wine cellar and she took off her little corduroy coat, she had the same flowered blouse on, only hers was made of fustian, not silk. But she wore a blue skirt like Candace. She didn't have a sweater on, although the ice crystals were bursting like firecrackers. Sidonia and her sisters had owned only one sweater among them, and that Sunday it was another sister's turn.

I said, "Professor Mather read a paper at the same conference. It was, in fact, an obituary for her late cousin Mortimer Pasternak. She had intimated to me that it would end in some sensational mathematical *pointe*. But it didn't."

The lovely girl at my side kicked a pebble lying on the path.

"Do you know who found the dead Pasternak in his office?"

She looked me straight in the eye: "Cooper?"

"Correct," I said. "And at that conference in Chicago, Cooper read his sensational paper, the day before Professor Mather. In the airplane, on our flight to Chicago, Mather told me that Pasternak, immediately before his death, had written her a moving letter."

We turned a curve, and there stood Dewey, sucking the lips of a man with a shaven head, his ears glittering with yellow mica. I hoped that Dewey had removed the ring from her lower lip for the occasion, but then I remembered she had discarded it a couple of days before because she loved pizza.

"The file cabinet in the studio of my colleague Mather was left open on a file labelled with the name you already know, Quentin."

She kept quiet. Now it was McMountain's turn to appear on the path, also with a beauty at his side. When they came nearer, I recognized Lorraine Henderson. No trace of mourning for her intended was to be seen in her lovely face. Quite soon. But *c'est la vie.*

"Correct me if I'm wrong, Quentin: you were eager to find out what Cooper was doing in Mather's house. You went around the house onto the terrace, and through the French window you saw Cooper standing at the opened cabinet. You started opening the French window, or inadvertently made a sound. I don't know, but you do. From a lighted room at night, however dimly lighted, one can't see what's going on outside. So you either made a sound or started opening the French window and Cooper panicked and ran away. You entered, saw the murdered Hammett, and then you noticed the half-opened file cabinet. You approached it, searched it and found the 'moving letter' from Professor Pasternak that Mather had mentioned to me on the plane. That was what Cooper was looking for when you startled him. At the time Pasternak had been writing the letter, however, there was nothing moving about it. It just *appeared* moving to his cousin after Pasternak's demise. Both Pasternak and Mather were mathematicians. They were very close to each other. What could be more natural than one cousin confiding to the other that he had discovered something? Later on, that something was to become the sensational *pointe* of Mather's paper in Chicago. But, in the end, there was no *pointe* whatever."

The college beauty grinned. "I suppose that now I should say, as culprits in *Murder, She Wrote* always do: 'You have no proof, professor!'" She was, as Yankees would say, a cool customer.

"Some I have, some I don't. Some are tangible, others intangible. One guesses at those by observing the behaviour of the suspect. Like, for instance, the sudden change in Cooper's evaluation of your mathematical prowess. Whatever is incomplete in my theory, you may complete yourself."

"I will, professor."

Her behaviour was uncharacteristic of detective stories. She should have kept silent and pierced me with hateful eyes, or she should have collapsed. Something like that. But we were not in a detective story—or were we? I at any rate was in a very serious novel, although Quentin didn't know that.

"You blackmailed Cooper, possibly because you'd caught him red-handed and then managed to flee—my wife commented to me after we'd dropped you off at your dorm that to judge by your appearance, you had just murdered someone— or you blackmailed him with the letter you'd found in Mather's file cabinet. It was probably a Xerox copy. Professor Mather kept the original in a safer place. But every Xerox copy must stem from an original and therefore, for your purpose, a Xerox sufficed. You held a knife to his throat, although all you wanted was an A-plus in his course. Not like Mary Mather, who wanted absolute revenge on her unfaithful husband. So she hired a murderer who came like a gift from above. She didn't pay him in cash. She remunerated him with the prospect of the Nobel Prize. If he hadn't accepted, she could have annihilated him in the academic community. Cooper is an ambitious snob and braggart; you can complete the rest of his personal characteristics, since you know him better than I do. He stole the paper that Pasternak had been preparing for the Chicago conference when he died. Mather had Pasternak's private letter and it did not contain just the usual phrases about how happy he was at his discovery. After all, they were both mathematicians. In that letter, Pasternak explained to his cousin the nature of his discovery. That was to be the *pointe* which Mary mentioned to me on the airplane. But on the first day of the conference, Cooper presented Pasternak's discovery as his own, and Mather knew that it was Cooper who had found her cousin lying dead with both his face and his theorem on his desk. At that time she was already thinking about some cruel and unusual punishment for her husband, who had so grossly disappointed her. And suddenly a gun for hire appeared like a gift from hell."

Silence. Then I said, "Oh yes. You must have spent quite a long time studying Professor Mather's file cabinet. Her husband was murdered about nine, you disturbed his murderer into fleeing shortly afterwards, yet my wife and I picked you up shortly after midnight. Another thing: when you found Pasternak's letter, how did you recognize its implications?"

Candace didn't answer. She was walking gracefully by my side, looking straight ahead.

"That was no problem," I answered myself. "Like Einstein's famous theory, Pasternak's theorem can also be expressed by a seemingly simple equation. Of course, only a few people understand it. But the college paper printed a special issue when the theorem created a sensation. You read it. Given your prowess in mathematics, you hardly knew what the theorem was about. But the paper's designer used the equation as an artfully designed symbol all through the paper. The same symbol you saw in Pasternak's letter to Professor Mather."

The next curve of the path revealed a scene similar to that in the Lame Duck when Wayne Hloupee had demonstrated how his voracious eating habits had disfigured the beautiful nude on his belly. A little crowd was standing on the path, with Sergeant Sayers turning round and round in its midst. She wore a brand-new, very girlish dress that fitted neatly around her slender waist, which she owed to the pill and celery sticks. Next to her, Wayne Hloupee towered in her old police uniform, which fitted him like his own skin. The ideas students had! At least in the country where Sidonia and I lived now. In the other country where we had lived once, students forged documents about their class origin and crammed the Teaching of All Teachings for the decisive exam of their lives. My friend Ludek Rus, a medical student in his last semester, had just gotten an A in forensic medicine, and then, straining all his mental muscles, successfully passed even the final and hardest exam in that Science to End All Sciences. It consisted of *The History of the All Union Communist Party of the Bolsheviks*, and had to be learned by heart. On February 26, 1956, the day after his exam, the Science to End All Sciences became invalid, because Nikita Khrushchev had so decided at the Twentieth Party Congress in the Kremlin. Ludek Rus had to take a replacement exam on Lenin's *Materialism and Empiriocriticism*, which he also managed to pass, but with a D.

The charming spectacle of youth soon vanished behind the maple trees. I said, "Whatever is missing from this final parade of facts and characters in the story, you can complete."

"I will, sir," she said, and remained silent.

Professor O'Sullivan appeared on the path, and gave us a once-over, her eyes filled with curiosity. She knew Quentin had dropped my course, and yet I was walking with her, all wrapped up in a conversation which looked confidential.

O'Sullivan, however, was no informer for the Sex Office, so my *tête-à-tête* with Candace would not be spread all over the campus like that rumour, that story, whatever it was.

"Will you tell on me?" Candace asked.

"I'm not sure. What if you confessed? You didn't *murder* Hammett. You only kept what you knew to yourself."

"Will I get expelled from the college?"

"Probably. That is, certainly."

Candace stopped. The spring breeze was ruffling her hair. She said, "Well, O.K. So I'll get married."

"But you wanted to study law, didn't you? You planned a professional career for yourself? The way you turned Cooper round your pinky convinces me that you would be a first-class lawyer."

She shrugged. "A first-class twister of facts, you mean." She grinned. "Oh, well. Never mind law school. I'll get married and have children."

And I remembered all those beautiful girls who had briefly shone like butterflies—then they had children, then they disappeared in the shadows of my memories. And I remembered Sidonia, who had no children and who would never disappear, as long as I would be able to remember.

"Think it over," I told Candace. "And see me tomorrow."

We parted.

WHETHER SHE CAME TO SEE ME THE NEXT DAY, I NEVER found out. When I came home, Sidonia was in a coma. Two empty bottles stood by her bed, and she was snow-white and unconscious. I called emergency, and I brought my wife to the hospital. There I sat in the waiting room, marking time while

172

I waited for the doctor to come and tell me that Sidonia was seriously ill.

All the years we had lived in the beautiful country which gave us a future, Sidonia had had a friend, Beryl. She was a professor of Russian, and before Sidonia learned English, Beryl would talk to her in the tongue of our enemies. She was almost old enough to be Sidonia's mother, and that's what she eventually became. Sidonia never had a mother like Beryl. Her own mother was a used-up woman, beaten and in the end killed by her Dickensian life in that country where omniscient evil gods knew even what she had once said in the butcher shop on Vitkova Street.

Years later Beryl moved to Virginia, where she and her husband got better jobs at the old university built by Jefferson. But they didn't move because of the better jobs. Beryl was an American and she was returning home. But you can't go home again. Once we came to Virginia to visit Sidonia's mother Beryl, and all that was left of the kind lady was a thin shadow, chain-smoking cigarettes. In a shed in the garden where she went to cut some flowers for the dining table, Sidonia discovered an immense number of empty half-gallon American liquor bottles. I went to see Beryl's husband, an old, retired professor who was unable to part with the university, and in his office he told me in a shaky voice, full of tears: "Her liver is gone!"

The door opened, the doctor appeared. I got up. The doctor told me in a matter-of-fact voice, "Her liver is gone."

SIDONIA LIVED FOR SOME MORE MONTHS. SHE WAS allowed one drink every evening, and from early morning she would fix her thoughts on that bright point of her day. Then, not even that. In my mind I kept playing that old film I had seen a thousand times, ten thousand times. How we criss-crossed the country where Beryl was born, thinking we had no future at all, though on that point we were wrong. It was a time when we still had no idea what lay ahead, and my old friend George Gibian arranged for a three-month job in Berkeley; there Sidonia sat day after day in the garden of the little house where we had rented a room, writing her beauti-ful novel. Day after day I would bring her a two-litre bottle of red wine, and then read her manuscript, and although I was young and unsentimental, I wept over its pages like an old man. It was Sidonia's wretched life: cruel, poor, ugly, because history had conspired against her. But with her writing, it had been changed into Keatsian joy. Forever. In our used DeSoto we then criss-crossed the lovely American land to Toronto, where Beryl managed to get me a one-year visiting lecture-ship. Since I had studied American literature, I remembered Hemingway's loss of his manuscripts, and night after night I would carry Sidonia's novel, written in longhand in American schoolchildren's exercise books, from our DeSoto to the motel in a grocery net bag of the kind no longer used in America. Then, thanks to the beautiful country where we now lived, happiness smiled on us. Late, but it did; and it is never too late to mend. During my holidays we would sail to the lovely Caribbean islands, where Sidonia could regain her strength. Then she would return to work in the publishing house, which she had founded and which she ran almost singlehand-edly until the day when the old regime in the country where we once had lived perished with a whimper. Then, from her old friend, now president, Sidonia received her Order. Then Mr. Mrkvicka printed the List.

A film I screened a hundred thousand times. While Sidonia was alive, the court hearing involving Mrs. Parsons never took place, because once again she did not show up, and so the trial was adjourned to the year 2000. However, Sidonia was no longer interested in those events: she lived for that one drink at dusk daily, then not even that. I was desperate. And I could do nothing.

THE POLICE NEVER FOUND THE MURDERER OF RAYMOND Hammett. Cooper accepted a chair at Harvard, where he never produced anything worth mentioning again. Mary Mather took early retirement and moved to Plymouth. Candace Quentin never told anyone what she knew. One year later she got married and still later she had beautiful children.

And I didn't tell anyone what I knew. One unpunished murderer more or less, who cares?

Redington Shores, Florida, February-March 1996
Deo gratias!